CONTENTS

THE HOTELIER'S BRIDE

The Balfour Hotel Book 2

AMANDA DAVIS

Can a plan to produce an heir, combined with a plan of deception and betrayal, lead to true love?

Xavier Balfour has an ugly envy simmering in his soul.
Each day, it grows like a weed wrapping its vines around the decency in his heart.

As Xavier watches his legacy fall into the hands of his sister's new husband,
He concocts a plan to produce an heir.

Entrusting his mother to play matchmaker,
It matters little to Xavy whom he weds.
The last thing he expects is to fall for Lady Elizabeth the moment he sets eyes upon her.

Elizabeth knows she cannot allow herself to indulge in feelings for her betrothed.
She and her mother, the Dutchess of Holden, have a plan of their own.
A plan that includes deception and, ultimately, betrayal.
A plan that does not include falling head over heels for the handsome Xavy Balfour.

PROLOGUE

It was unbecoming, the ugly envy that seemed to be simmering inside Xavier's soul. Each day, it grew like a weed, suffocating, wrapping its vines around the decency in his heart and reducing him to a glowering shadow of his former self.

Xavier was aware of it, of course. It was difficult to ignore, after all, yet there was little he could do to sate it.

It is nearly impossible with Emmeline bringing that outsider into our family affairs.

He longed to be happy for her, the new life his sister had brought into the hotel casting a ray of light over his dismal thoughts. But, even with the new arrival of his niece, Xavier Balfour could not suppress the overwhelming disappointment at the turn of events that had led his legacy to fall into the hands of Elias Compton.

You are being ridiculous, he chided himself. *Elias is your brother-in-law now.*

Nothing seemed to stifle the mounting resentment inside him and, as the days passed, January faded into early February, but the promise of spring was still long off.

Xavier grew increasingly restless.

He was a tall man, Xavier. Strangely so, considering the height of his father and mother, but it did distinguish him from others in his presence. With a sweeping mane of blond hair and emerald eyes, he was oft the center of talk among the ladies who vied for his attention. That day was no different as he glided swiftly through the lobby, nodding amiably despite the anger burning in his chest.

"Good morrow, Mr. Balfour," Matthew called from the concierge desk.

"Is my father present?" Xavier asked, rudely ignoring Matthew's greeting. But Matthew seemed accustomed to the brusqueness and nodded pleasantly.

"Indeed, sir. Shall I announce you?"

"You need not bother. I will do it myself."

Without giving Matthew an opportunity to react, he entered his father's office, sans indication of his arrival.

Charlton Balfour scowled from behind his massive desk.

"You of all should know better than to interrupt a man when he is working."

"I see you are alone," Xavier commented without addressing his father's annoyance. "Where is Elias?"

"I sent him off to spend time with Emmy and the baby."

Xavier grunted obtusely and narrowed his eyes.

"Women have been bearing children for centuries," he reminded his father. "It is the man's task to work."

"Xavier, is there a matter that you came to discuss, or are you merely here to recount your displeasure that Elias is now part owner of the hotel?"

Xavier's jaw locked defiantly.

He dismisses me now that Elias is here. As if that peasant could possibly provide better for the hotel that bears my family's name than I.

At that moment, Xavier realized what it was that had been troubling him, the elusive point he had been unable to identify.

Elias has replaced you in Father's eyes.

"Xavier!" Charlton snapped, his patience wearing thin. "What is the matter? Out with it, please. I have much work to attend to today."

Xavier lifted his head, his eyes meshing with the older man's.

"I have decided to marry," he announced, and Charlton's brow shot up in bemused surprise.

"Marriage? You?" he chortled. "Who is the unsuspecting wench?"

Xavier bristled at the crass language.

"Do you think so poorly of me that you think I would wed beneath our status?" he demanded.

"My son, I do not claim to know the first thing about what you would do in this situation," Charlton chuckled. "I do believe this is the first time I have ever heard you use the word 'marriage' without cringing."

"A man can change, Father," Xavier insisted. "Perhaps I am inspired by what Emmeline has found in Elias."

"Inspired or envious, Xavy?"

Xavier tensed but willed himself to remain composed.

"Father, we must regain control of the Balfour Hotel—the Balfours, not some outsider."

"I have control of the hotel," Charlton reminded him, but Xavier did not miss the shadow that fell over his father's face.

He did not feel confident in selling to Elias, either, but what choice did he have?

"They already have one child," Xavier murmured softly. "We are fortunate it is a girl, but what if Emmy births sons?"

"It does not change the fact that we still own the majority of the hotel," Charlton reminded him. "What can we do about it if they birth a litter of boys?"

"Boys become men, and men become greedy," Xavier hissed. "Look at how Elias has stepped—"

Charlton raised a hand to silence his son.

"I must admit, I am growing weary listening to the same tired argument, Xavier. What is it you wish from me?"

"I want for you to arrange a match for me."

Charlton scoffed and eyed Xavier with mild contempt.

"This might be a task better suited to your mother, Xavier," he muttered, and it was Xavier's turn to be dubious.

"Mother?" he echoed. "Father, I do not think—"

"Xavier, I have a business to attend to. I cannot submit to your whimsy because you are in competition with Elias. From all I have gleaned, he is a good man with pure intentions."

A good man who has blinded both my sister and my father while taking what is rightfully ours.

Xavier did not speak the words aloud. After all, they would not have been in such a position if Charlton had not put the family at such risk.

"Speak to your mother if you are sincere in your desire to find a wife," Charlton told him dismissively. "It will do her good to focus on something other than..."

He did not finish his thought, but he did not need to complete his statement—Xavier knew what it was that plagued his mother, Anne.

"Is there another matter, Xavy?"

The question was a dismissal, but Xavier did not move.

"Father?" he asked, and Charlton grunted quietly.

"Yes?"

"Does Elias's presence here not trouble you in the least?"

Charlton raised his eyes to meet his son's, his lips tightening.

"Until he gives me cause for concern, I have little say in the matter," Charlton replied, but it told Xavier much in so few words.

He is no happier about Elias than I am. We must find a way to see him out of his shares and reclaim the family legacy back into our hands.

"Xavier, if there is nothing else..."

"I will speak to Mother," Xavier replied, nodding curtly. "Good day."

Charlton did not bother to respond, and the younger Balfour shifted toward the door to leave the proprietor in peace.

Father may be passive in this intrusion to our family, but I will not stand by and permit it to happen. It is on my shoulders to save this family.

As he hurried from the office toward the broad, winding staircase, Xavier paused, guilt flooding him instantly.

His sister slowly descended, a bundle of blankets in her arms as her handmaiden fluttered nearby awkwardly.

At her side, Elias took her arm, and for a moment, Xavier felt as though he was staring at a painting, rather than his family.

"Good morrow, Xavier!" Emmeline breathed, her face still pale from the experience of childbearing, but there was most certainly a happy glow about her, which had not been there before the birth.

"Good morrow, Emmy," he murmured, slipping forward to steal a glance at the baby in her arms. He all but ignored Elias, who had yet to speak.

"How is our princess faring?" Xavier asked.

"She is perfect," Emmeline sighed, her eyes twinkling. "Would you care to hold her?"

Xavier shook his head and laughed, stepping back.

"I would not know how," he chuckled.

"Mrs. Compton, I am pleased to take her," Cora muttered, looking uncomfortable that her mistress held the baby at all.

"As I have told you several times already, Cora, I am quite capable of holding my own child."

Cora balked and lowered her eyes, wringing her hands against the crisp white of her apron.

"You should rest," Elias told his wife tenderly, reaching for baby Catherine. With shocked eyes, Xavier watched his sister hand the bundle of white blankets to her husband.

The nanny stands at their side! What will the guests think if they see him handling the baby?

It was merely one more reason for Xavier to think poorly of his new brother-in-law.

He does not know his place. He thinks he is still a shop owner in Peterborough, not the proprietor of a luxurious hotel. Elias will drag down our prestige with his uncouth ways.

"I have done little else than rest for a fortnight!" Emmeline complained. "I want to be up again, working in the hotel."

The words sent a small sliver of apprehension through Xavier. When Emmeline resumed her duties, Elias certainly would also.

And it will be that much more difficult to hide my intentions.

"I believe you should listen to your husband," Xavier said crisply.

"Father and I have matters under control while you take the time you require to recover fully. You would not want to fall ill."

"Xavier is correct, Emmeline. There is nothing that your brother and I cannot handle with your father."

Xavier's jaw locked, and he glanced furtively at Elias, but the man's eyes were fixed on the face of his infant daughter.

A now-familiar stone formed in the base of Xavier's chest as he stared balefully at Elias.

He has everything that I deserve, he realized, the hot jealousy sweeping through him again. *The hotel, my father's appreciation, a wife and a child.*

It was stunning to the dashing and charming Xavier that such a wave of envy could consume him when he watched Elias, yet he knew it was precisely what he felt.

Not for long, he vowed. *Soon I will be better off than Elias.*

"Are you well, Xavy?" Emmeline asked with concern. "You seem positively enraged."

Quickly, he forced a smile and shook his head.

"Not in the least," he replied. "I must go, however. I must speak with Mother."

Emmeline's eyebrows shot up.

"Mother?" she echoed. "What about?"

Xavier's smile widened, more sincerity piping through the curve of his mouth.

"It is a secret," he replied in a staged whisper, his eyes glittering mischievously, and Emmeline giggled.

"Why does that cause my heart to race with concern?" she asked while he beamed at her. "Your secrets are infamously worrisome."

"The news is good," he promised her, his smile fading slightly as he considered, for the first time, what his plan might do to his sister.

She is still a Balfour, Xavier reminded himself. *She does not need Elias when she has us.*

"I must go," Xavier continued, nodding at her and again ignoring Elias.

"Good luck with Mother," Emmeline whispered, her dark-lashed eyes darting about to ensure she had not been overheard.

Good luck, indeed, Xavier thought grimly, climbing the stairs toward

Anne's bedchambers. *I am putting my future into the hands of a drunk, after all.*

Yet it did not stop Xavier from making his way to her suite and knocking gently on the door to announce himself.

I would rather be matched by Mother's inebriated hand than watch the Balfour Hotel fall into Elias Compton's.

Xavier's only hope was that he would not lose his beloved sister when Elias was forced to leave.

CHAPTER ONE

The glass about the conservatory panes had frosted, making a look outside impossible.

Lise was quite certain her mother had arranged the setting purposely, knowing that there would be no way for her daughter to see who was approaching. It was a sound move on the part of the duchess, but Lady Elizabeth Burnaby was a near wreck of nerves as she sat shivering in the glass house.

Most of the greenery had perished in the frigid winter temperature, but one strong vine had survived, and Lise found herself staring at it for inspiration to guide her through the next moments.

What is the meaning of this secrecy? Why could we not attend this interview inside the manor?

They were questions she could only ask her mother, but the Duchess of Holden had been conspicuously absent all morning, leaving Lise to follow the housekeeper through the icy fields into the conservatory.

Bernadette stood by quietly, but even in her steadfast stoicism, Lise could feel the servant's eyes upon her.

"What is the hour, Bernadette?" Lise asked, trying to keep the words from trembling in her speech.

"Just before eleven, Lady Elizabeth."

"What is keeping her?" Lise snapped with a great deal more irritability than she had intended. "I have been here for a quarter hour already!"

"Shall I fetch you a cup of tea, Lady Elizabeth?"

Instinctively, Lise wrapped her cloak about her shoulders and wrenched her eyes away from the thriving plant to stare almost angrily at Bernadette as though she was somehow to blame for the situation.

"I would rather that you fetch the duchess," Lise replied shortly. She barely had a moment to process the flash of uncertainty in Bernadette's eyes when the door opened and Duchess Holden entered in a sweeping air of grace and poise.

Lise's mother stopped to gape at her daughter in surprise.

"It is quite cold in here!" Duchess Holden announced, and Lise's brow raised in shock.

"Is that stunning, Mother?" she demanded. "It is the month of February, and we have not a hearth in here."

"Bernadette, fetch a pot of tea at once. Our guest will be arriving shortly, and these accommodations will not do!"

Lise was almost grateful that they would, at the minimum, be returning indoors, but to her chagrin, the Duchess only moved further into the structure as Bernadette curtsied and scurried away to oblige her request.

"Mother, what is the meaning of this?" Lise asked in exasperation. "Why must we meet here?"

Duchess Holden did not reply and instead glided toward the cast iron table set where she gently perched upon a small chair.

"You need not be dramatic, my dear," her mother replied as she adjusted her gloves uncomfortably. It was plain to see that she was as cold as Lise, but her face did not betray an iota of what she was thinking.

"I am cold, Mother."

Duchess Holden scowled.

"Use your patience, Lise. Why do you think I have chosen such a discrete meeting place?"

A shiver coursed through Lise, but it had little to do with the temperature.

"Mother, what have you done?" Lise whispered, her slate-gray eyes darting toward the door, lest Bernadette return.

Patience stared blankly at her second child, her mouth becoming a fine line of disapproval.

"I suspect you know fully what this is about," she hissed. "You will not embarrass me when she arrives."

"*She?*" Lise echoed. The matter was becoming stranger with each spoken word.

"Yes. His mother."

Their eyes met, and a fusion of worry and relief flowed through Lise. She slowly moved toward the table where the duchess sat nonchalantly.

She intends to see this through. All of our discussions on the matter were not as fruitless as I expected.

Fear overcame all other emotions, and she turned her attention back to the duchess.

"Who are they?" Lise asked quietly.

"You will find out soon enough."

"Mother, please. I cannot go blindly into this—"

"That is entirely the point, is it not?"

Lise stifled a sigh.

"I am not being contrary, Mother," she murmured. "You cannot fault me for being curious."

"You will not be contrary," the duchess replied, raising her eyes to meet Lise's. "Not if you wish for this to work. You should be seen and not heard today."

Lise bristled.

"I am hardly a child, Mother," she countered. "I need not—"

"Lise," Patience interrupted crossly. "The matter is not for discussing. You will simply listen and not speak. It is important that she appreciate your beauty, if nothing else. She need not get a glimpse of your inquisitive nature, Lise. It will be our downfall."

Lise frowned, but she knew her mother was correct. Oh, how she wished she could portray herself as the coy women she saw at parties, batting their eyelashes and discussing nonsense, but it was not in her nature when her desire was to learn.

Unfortunately, it was not a quality that men found desirable and, no matter how Lise tried to suppress the endless queries from spilling forth, her curiosity inevitably got the best of her.

There is far too much at stake for me to upset the apple cart in this instance. I will be silent and permit Mother to do whatever it is she has planned.

Gooseflesh prickled Lise's skin, but there was nothing else to say as the door opened again and Bernadette hurried back into the conservatory with a pot of tea.

"Your Grace," the servant muttered nervously. "Your visitor has arrived. Shall I see her through here?"

The duchess eyed Bernadette with scorn.

"It is freezing in the conservatory!" she replied haughtily. "I could not see a guest in here. See her to the front parlor. We will be along in a moment."

Confusion colored Bernadette's cheeks, and Lise realized then that her mother had only wished to forewarn her privately before the arrival of the lady. The servants' ears were everywhere in a manor, and her mother had been wise to ensure their seclusion.

"As you wish, Your Grace," Bernadette muttered, perplexed, but she set the tray down and hurried back out the door.

"Who is it, Mother?" Lise asked when she was certain Bernadette had escaped earshot. "What is her name?"

"Mrs. Anne Balfour."

Lise's brow furrowed as she tried to remember the name, but it seemed to tantalize the recesses of her mind somehow.

"I cannot say I know her."

"She is the wife of a wealthy hotel proprietor in Luton, very much a recluse from what I understand."

"And her son?"

Patience nodded, her clear blue eyes meeting Lise's.

"Xavier. Quite handsome from what I have learned."

Mother and daughter shared a long, silent stare, each thinking the same dark but hopeful thoughts.

We must solidify this union if we wish to survive.

————

"Duchess, Lady Elizabeth, may I present Mrs. Anne Balfour of Luton. Mrs. Balfour, Her Grace, Patience, Duchess of Holden, and her daughter, Lady Elizabeth Burnaby."

The frail, waxen-faced woman rose to curtsey before the mother and daughter, her head lowered respectfully. There were remnants of what had once been a stunningly lovely face beneath a hardened shell, which somehow contrasted the plaintive expression on her face.

She seemed both breakable and invincible, hard and vulnerable.

"Your Grace, Lady Elizabeth, I thank you for receiving me," she murmured, and Lise glanced at her mother, wondering if the duchess heard what she had.

She recalled her vow to hold her tongue but her mother refused to meet her gaze, making Lise's promise so much more difficult.

"Please, do sit," Patience told her. Suter stood nearby, awaiting instructions, and the duchess nodded to him as Mrs. Balfour reclaimed her spot upon the velvet settee.

"Suter, send for tea," she instructed, and the butler nodded, vanishing into the vast manor house.

"You have a lovely home, Your Grace," Mrs. Balfour offered. "One of the finest I have seen."

"I understand your hotel caters to the upperclassmen," Patience replied. "I am certain you are no stranger to luxury."

"Luxury, perhaps not. Opulence is quite another matter."

Lise's eyes widened at the veiled insult, but to her surprise, Patience laughed.

"I concur. The duke does tend to overfill a chamber with his golden trinkets. Some men will compensate for their own shortcomings in various ways, I imagine. Surely you can relate, Mrs. Balfour."

To add to Lise's amazement, Mrs. Balfour also chuckled.

"Indeed," she agreed, as Suter shuffled back into the parlor with a shining silver tray in his hands.

Silently, the butler poured the tea for the ladies, and they each eyed one another speculatively.

"You do not say much, my lady," Mrs. Balfour commented. "Are you shy? It would be a terrible shame if you had no wit to accompany that comely face."

Lise looked at her mother and swallowed the lump of nervousness in her windpipe.

"I am not shy, Mrs. Balfour. Perhaps a tad anxious."

"That is to be expected in these situations, but I can assure you, Lady Elizabeth, my son is not a man to be feared. The ladies find him to be all the crack, and I am told he takes after me with his fairness and eyes."

Lise tried with all her might to envision a masculine form of the waif before her, but it did not form well in her imagination.

She managed a small smile.

"I am certain he is dashing, Mrs. Balfour."

Anne leaned forward, her emerald irises bloodshot and glazed.

"I daresay you will make beautiful children," she murmured, and Lise was shocked by her forwardness. She turned her head to look helplessly at her mother, but Patience had busied herself with her cup and saucer, leaving Lise's face to flush crimson.

"I did not mean to embarrass you, Lady Elizabeth," Anne told her worriedly. "Forgive my frankness."

"No need to apologize, Mrs. Balfour," Patience interjected before Lise could respond. "I am just as eager as you to hear the pitter-patter of small feet."

Once more, the women exchanged a smile, and Lise's gut twisted into knots of concern as she watched the farce unfolding before her.

"Shall we make arrangements to visit Luton?" Patience asked some time later, sensing that Anne Balfour was growing restless in the house.

"Indeed!" Mrs. Balfour agreed, seeming relieved that they had taken to her. "If you inform me of when you intend to arrive, I will see to the arrangements."

"Perhaps we can come tomorrow?" the duchess suggested, and Lise's mouth fell slightly apart.

Before Father returns from London? Will he not be enraged that we are gone?

"T-tomorrow?" Anne echoed.

"Will that be a matter?"

"No! Certainly not. I will ensure you have a suite on the fifth floor. Xavier will be beside himself with excitement to meet you, Lady Elizabeth."

"We, too, look forward to seeing your renowned hotel, Mrs. Balfour."

"Shall we expect the duke?"

"Unfortunately, matters in London detain him."

"Will he not wish to know if they choose to become engaged?" Anne insisted, and for the first time, Lise saw a glimmer of intelligence in her dull, green eyes.

"Of course," the duchess answered without missing one beat of the conversation. "But he extends his blessings through me, I assure you."

"Of course," Anne muttered.

"If it is the dowry that concerns you, Mrs. Balfour..."

"Certainly not!" The woman seemed offended by the suggestion and met Patience's stare evenly. "The Balfours want for nothing, Your Grace."

"If I thought that was the case, I would have never agreed to this match," Patience replied, and there seemed to be an uneasy truce between the ladies—for the time being.

Anne rose to her feet and curtsied quickly.

"Until tomorrow then," she said, her smile watery.

"Indeed," Patience agreed. "Good day, Mrs. Balfour. Thank you for your attendance."

Anne was shown from the parlor, and Lise whirled to look at her mother, the lace hem of her skirts swirling at her ankles.

"She was drunk!" Lise choked. "Did you smell the spirits on her?"

"She was a trifle disguised," Patience agreed. "I thought to offer her sherry or port, but I feared she might never leave."

"Does that not trouble you? That my mother-in-law is a drunk?"

Patience chuckled mirthlessly.

"Oh, my sweet, naïve child," she snickered. "You will understand the ways of women much better when you are wed."

"Mother—"

Patience lost her bemused expression, her face hardening.

"It is for the best," she snapped, lowering her voice to a low hiss. "If she is drunk often, she will be far too consumed with herself to be fretting about you. I cannot tell you how trying it has been to find a match who is not closely related to the duchy yet who carries the means we require."

Reluctantly, Lise had to agree with her mother even though her doubts were growing as they spoke.

She may not be a lady of sound mind, but Mrs. Balfour does not seem to be cruel. Will I be able to see this through?

Queerly, she hoped that Xavier Balfour was a brute or somehow unworthy of her compassion.

"Do you understand what I am saying, Lise?" the duchess insisted, and Lise sighed, bobbing her head.

"Yes," she murmured.

The fewer eyes I have upon my actions, the less likely it is I will be caught when I am forced to betray them all.

CHAPTER TWO

"Today, Mother? You cannot be sincere!"

Xavier gazed at Anne in disbelief, but she seemed unperturbed by his outburst.

"Why not today?" she asked, her words almost slurring as she brushed her flaxen hair in the vanity.

"Who is she? Why did you not mention that you were already pursuing matches? Why, I only came to you with this information a week ago!"

"When you did come, Xavier, I expected that you intended to marry. Have you changed your mind?"

"I-no," he sputtered, feeling quite drunk himself at that moment. "Of course, I have not changed my mind, Mother. I simply would have preferred to be consulted before you brought a duke and his daughter here for a betrothal."

"The duke will not be here," Anne intoned. "It will be the Duchess of Holden and Lady Elizabeth."

"Why?" Xavier exploded. "What is the purpose if the duke is not present?"

"Her Grace assures me that she has authority to accept the terms of a betrothal if you should find the lady becoming enough."

A thousand words of protest formed on Xavier's lips but died there just as quickly when he realized that he should be grateful, not alarmed.

It was merely so sudden. He had not expected an appointment so quickly.

Alas, time is wasting while Elias eyes the hotel. What is it you await?

"She is charming, in a quiet way," Anne explained. "She will be a stunning contrast on your arm with her ebony locks, I daresay."

Anne turned and eyed him warily.

"She is the daughter of a duke, Xavier."

"So you have said," Xavier replied, his interest in Lady Elizabeth growing.

"I do not think you understand, my dear," Anne barked with unusual sharpness and Xavier could see that despite her constant state of inebriation, she still had her wits about her.

"Enlighten me, Mother. What is it you are attempting to say?"

"You must stop your whoremongering ways," Anne told him bluntly. "I know you are on too-familiar terms with every abbess from here to Cambridge."

Xavier's face blushed crimson.

"That is categorically untrue!" Xavier lied, confounded as to how his reclusive mother could know of his lewd interests. Anne seemed unmoved by his protests, a fact that only inflamed his cheeks more.

"Xavier, I have fashioned this match for you because you have asked. You will do no better than a lady of such high standing, but if you cannot control yourself—"

"Mother!" he cut in sharply. "I will adhere to my wedding vows."

He wondered if she could hear the doubt in his own words, and he was filled with shame as he thought it.

"We will see, I imagine," Anne sighed, and Xavier knew he was fooling no one with his proclamations.

Perhaps she will be the one who captures my heart, Xavier thought and snickered at the notion. He was not so naïve to believe that any union in which he found himself would be borne of emotion. It was merely a necessity, free of any sentiment.

"I am pleased to see this amuses you so well," Anne said curtly.

"I am not amused, Mother," he assured her. "I am happily antici-pating the arrival of Lady Elizabeth."

Anne grunted and waved him away as though he was a gnat trou-bling her.

"I should never have agreed to this. You will shame us all with your amorous intentions."

"I will do no such thing," Xavier growled, resentful that his mother thought so poorly of him. "My loyalty has always been to the hotel and this family. I would never jeopardize our reputation."

Anne studied him silently for a long while and nodded slowly.

"Perhaps," she murmured. "Perhaps."

"When will they arrive? I must make myself presentable."

"I cannot say. They did not specify, but it is not a long journey from Holden."

"Then I will ensure I am there to greet them when they arrive. Shall I meet you in the lobby, Mother?"

Anne looked at him in surprise.

"I will not be there," she replied, an air of confusion about her. "My duty in this matter is complete."

He balked and shook his head.

"How will I know who they are?"

Anne smiled faintly.

"You will know," she assured him in her strange, wise way.

———

Matthew watched him covertly as Xavier paced through the lobby, barely unable to contain his growing excitement.

He wished the concierge would not stare at him, but he was aware that he must be quite a sight, donned in a rather conspicuous wardrobe choice at such an early hour of the morning.

Anne's words echoed through his mind.

I must make a decent impression if I wish to win the hand of a lady.

His mother had given him little in the way of expectation, only that he would be pleased with her match.

"Matthew," Xavier asked impatiently. "Have you nothing better to do than gawk at the proprietor this morning?"

Matthew balked and lowered his eyes guiltily.

"Forgive me, Mr. Xavier. I-I was merely admiring your attire."

"Admire it whilst working," Xavier retorted, but he was secretly flattered by the appreciation, if only by an employee.

"Yes, sir."

He shifted his eyes downward, and Xavier's attention moved toward the dining room where Samuel, the new maître d', was overseeing the waiters.

He is not new, Xavier corrected himself. *He has been here for almost one year.*

It was hard to reconcile that Honor, the man in his previous position, was gone. Honor had been with the hotel since his birth, and a newcomer to the position was still a difficult matter for Xavier to accept.

Yet another reason to fault Elias. As though I needed more cause to protest his presence.

Antoinette appeared at Samuel's side, and Xavier noted with mild interest that they seemed to be speaking very closely.

He idly wondered if Samuel and the head of housekeeping were more than simple acquaintances.

Antoinette seemed to feel his gaze upon her, and she looked toward him, a flash of shame appearing on her face.

"Good morrow, Mr. Xavier," Antoinette said, lowering her head nervously.

"Good morrow, Antoinette, Samuel."

The maître d' nodded curtly, respectfully and skilfully avoiding his eyes.

"You look dashing, sir, if you do not mind me being so bold. May I ask the occasion?"

Xavier flushed slightly but maintained his composure, shaking his blond head of hair.

"He is meeting his wife," Emmeline gushed from his side, and Xavier whirled in shock. He had not realized that his sister was nearby.

"Mind yourself!" he barked with unexpected force. Emmeline's smile faded, and she seemed perplexed by his reaction.

"Is it not true?" she asked, tipping her fair face to the side. "I was told—"

"By whom? What were you told?"

Emmeline's expression took on a look of discomfort.

"Mother asked me to join you in meeting the duchess and Lady Elizabeth," she replied, and it was only then that Xavier noticed how properly his sister was dressed also.

"I-I do not need an escort, Emmy!" he hissed, looking toward Antoinette, who had the good sense to leave the siblings alone.

"It is not a matter of escorting you, my dear brother," Emmeline replied. "Consider it a form of support."

"Emmeline, this is unnecessary."

"Mother does not seem to think so," Emmeline insisted, and he found himself marveling at her unabashed insistence.

"Mother should be here herself if the matter is so important to her. Where is the infant?"

"With the nanny. Catherine will fare well without me for a short luncheon."

"I would rather you did not..."

He had barely gotten the words out when the double doors opened and two manservants entered in a bustle of trunks.

Xavier and Emmeline exchanged a look.

"Could they have arrived?" Emmeline asked, but her brother was already moving toward the outdoor rotunda to look onto the path below where a coach and six had appeared.

Mother was right—it is quite difficult to overlook such a display.

A handsome woman stood smartly at the base of the steps, a broadly brimmed hat shielding her face from the shocking February sunshine. She seemed to be examining the five stories of the hotel with impassioned eyes, and she had yet to see Xavier standing on the stone just to the right of her sightline.

That would be the duchess, he thought, his eyes darting about to seek out her daughter.

"Oh my," Emmeline breathed at his side, and he turned to look where she did. With the same emotion that he had heard in his sister's voice, Xavier's heart seemed to cease its beats when his eyes fell upon who could only be Lady Elizabeth Burnaby.

A thick, woolen cloak of blue accented the porcelain of her delicate skin. Despite the distance between them, Xavier could see the gleam of long, black curls bouncing slowly as Elizabeth looked about with awe in a pair of wide, smoky eyes.

"She is breathtaking," Emmeline murmured at his side. "I find myself envious of such a complexion."

Xavier could not tear his gaze away, and slowly, Elizabeth's eyes rested on his face.

A shadow of surprise covered her eyes, and for a peaceful, strange moment, Xavier thought all else had disappeared. There were only two of them in the world, and they were lost in one another.

"Xavier, you must attend to them," Emmeline whispered, shattering the short spell that had fallen between her brother and the duke's daughter.

"Yes," he mumbled. "Of course."

Offering Emmeline his arm, the two glided down the steps toward the new arrivals. With great effort, he directed his words to the matriarch, difficult as it was when he could feel Elizabeth's eyes upon him.

"Welcome to the Balfour Hotel, Your Grace, Lady Elizabeth," he offered genially, his eyes fixed on Elizabeth. "I am Xavier Balfour, and this is my sister, Mrs. Emmeline Compton."

Xavier bowed graciously.

"Mr. Balfour, Mrs. Compton."

The duchess gave him a quick appraisal before nodding.

"I daresay, I was expecting your mother, Mr. Balfour."

"You must forgive her absence, Your Grace," Xavier replied smoothly, well-accustomed to making excuses for Anne's endless absences. "She is unwell."

The look that the duchess and her daughter shared was not lost on Xavier, yet neither made a comment on the matter.

"Do come in and out of the cold," Emmeline suggested, disentangling her arm from her brother's. "I will arrange to have your trunks brought to your suite. I hope you will find our hotel accommodating."

"Yes," Elizabeth said, speaking for the first time, and the husky sound of her voice again caused Xavier's heart to flutter. "I am certain we will find all we need here."

Once more, the duchess and Elizabeth shared a private look, but Xavier barely noticed. His pulse raced erratically through his veins in a way he had never known.

Perhaps this marriage would exceed his expectations after all.

CHAPTER THREE

"What is keeping you, Lise?" Patience demanded. "We are expected in the dining room."

Lise stood before the vanity, examining her reflection with a scrutiny she did not recognize.

Am I as beautiful as his eyes told me?

The memory of Xavier's bright green irises boring into her was not one she was apt to forget. Had there ever been another to give her such a brazen yet intense look?

What does he see?

"My word, Lise! Vanity is a sin!" the duchess snapped. "Have you had quite enough of gawking at yourself?"

A blush of humiliation flooded Lise's cheeks, and she turned to her mother.

"I was merely ensuring I look presentable," she replied meekly.

"You were sure a quarter hour ago. Moreover, you could wear a sack of potatoes and that fool would not be the wiser."

More heat tinged Lise's face.

"Whatever do you mean?"

Patience scoffed lightly and unavoidably examined herself in the glass.

"Dismissed," she told the two maids hovering nearby, and the women disappeared without a word, leaving the mother and daughter alone in their spacious suite.

While Lise had never had occasion to sleep in a hotel, she admitted that it was quite lavish. Certainly, it exceeded what she had envisioned.

"I am not blind, child. I saw how he looked at you," Duchess Holden said sharply, and Lise's ears heated at the reminder.

"I did not notice," Lise fibbed, and Patience whipped her head to stare at her daughter with knit brows.

"You did, and you requite those sentiments. Not that I fault you— Anne Balfour did not lie; her son is quite dashing, even for a dandyish fop."

"He is not a fop!" Lise protested before she could stop herself.

"Aha!" the duchess growled. "So I am correct. You find him charming."

"I find him nothing!" Lise wished she could contain the passion in her voice, but it appeared to be beyond her control. "I have not forgotten why we have come, Mother."

Patience stared at her for a long while, her mouth pinched in at the sides.

"There is no harm in feeling warmth for him, Lise," her mother said quietly. "In fact, I would much prefer it for your task. It would make the ordeal so much less daunting if you like the man you are to wed."

Lise lowered her eyes and stared at the white gloves on her hands.

"However," Patience continued. "You must not grow too attached."

"I am aware, Mother."

Patience paused.

"Lise, if you do not wish to proceed with this, I will understand," her mother said quietly. "It is unfair that you should carry the burden of such a task on your shoulders alone."

Lise raised her head and stared intently into her mother's sad eyes.

"No, Mother," she sighed, shaking her ebony tresses, one rogue curl falling against the pale skin of her cheek. "This is our burden to bear together. I will not change my mind on the matter."

A soft, melancholic smile touched the duchess's lips, and she nodded slowly.

"You are a good daughter, Lise, but I oft wish you had been born first and a male."

"There is little I can do to change God's will, Mother, but I will do whatever I can to protect you."

"It is a mother's duty to shield her young from the hardships of life."

"We are nobility, Mother," Lise commented with sardonic dryness. "We are not supposed to know hardships."

"Yet we do, do we not? Better than most, I would say."

Despair swept through Lise, but she was determined not to show her mother her sadness.

"You need not concern yourself with my affections for Xavier Balfour," she assured her mother, "for I have none."

If possible, the duchess seemed more crestfallen by the announcement, but she fronted a brave smile.

"Shall we go?" Patience asked, and Lise could see she was eager to shift the conversation.

"Yes," Lise agreed.

———

The dining room was surprisingly full for the off-season, and Lise found herself wondering from where all the upperclassmen had come. She could not reconcile why so many finely dressed ladies and gentlemen flocked to the somewhat obscure location of the hotel.

Some faces were vaguely familiar as she looked about. Certainly, the Balfour Hotel catered only to the highest echelons of society, and that fact both alarmed and pleased Lise in unison.

She mentioned her concerns to her mother.

"Surely we will be recognized, even here," she muttered as they were guided to the family's table where Xavier, Emmeline, and another two men waited for them with barely disguised patience.

"You need not concern yourself with the duke," Duchess Holden told her softly. "I have explained that we will be grooming you for marriage."

Lise's eyes widened. She had not known that the duke knew that much.

"The Balfours," Patience breathed, and Lise raised her eyes as they neared the table at the guide of the maître d'.

"Your Grace, Lady Elizabeth," Xavier announced, rising with the men in unison. "Permit me to introduce my father, Mr. Charlton Balfour, proprietor of this fine establishment. Father, may I present, Patience, Duchess of Holden, and Lady Elizabeth Burnaby, her daughter."

"Charmed," Patience said, nodding politely at the man.

"Please to make your acquaintance," Lise breathed as the men bowed.

"You have already met my sister, Mrs. Emmeline Compton," Xavier continued, and his face hardened as he introduced the last man in improper order. "This is her husband, Mr. Elias Compton."

"My husband also holds shares in the hotel," Emmeline offered, and Xavier's scowl deepened.

There seems to be some animus. I wonder if that will help us or hurt us.

Elias seemed unperturbed by Xavier's curt and somewhat inappropriate introduction, and he bowed to the ladies where they stood.

"Welcome to the Balfour Hotel, Your Grace, my lady."

Xavier gestured for everyone to sit, and the waiters held chairs for the newcomers to join the table.

"Your hotel is quite charming, Mr. Balfour," the duchess offered as wine was poured. "Our accommodations were precisely as Mrs. Balfour promised—exceptional."

Charlton Balfour's chest puffed out with pride, and he nodded.

"It has been in our family for generations," Charlton explained. "We take great pride in this structure."

"Until now," Xavier muttered almost under his breath. No one seemed to hear his offhanded remark but Lise, and that was merely because she had been unable to tear her eyes from his face.

I must stop staring at him so brazenly. He will think of me as some fallen woman.

She darted her eyes away and tried to heed the conversation around her, but inevitably, her stare would fall on his face, and he would meet her eyes, too.

"Where is the Duke of Holden?" Charlton asked quite pointedly, and Lise wrenched her face toward her mother's expression. It was alarming how easily she maintained her stoicism, despite the way her heart must be racing.

"He has urgent business in London," she explained, reaching for her glass. "He sends his regards, of course. And how is Mrs. Balfour?"

She asked with such smooth transition, Lise marveled at her flawless manner of reversing her discomfort on the Balfours. Simultaneously, the family looked away in a breath of discomfort.

"She has a delicate disposition," Charlton offered tersely, and Lise did not need to be told that her initial impression of Anne Balfour had been accurate.

She is a drunk. How unfortunate for the family.

Yet she knew better than to judge the affairs of another family, not when her own house was in such disarray.

"I do hope she recovers well," the duchess replied, sitting back as a plate was delivered to her setting.

"She will," they chorused and exchanged embarrassed looks. Once more, Xavier's eyes fell on Lise, and she reddened slightly.

"How long will you stay with us?" Emmeline asked, apparently hoping to shift the conversation. "There is much to do in Luton despite the frigid temperature."

"That would depend on Mr. Xavier, I imagine," Patience replied, lowering her fork. "How long will it take for him to fashion a proposal?"

The gasp of surprise over the table was warranted and included Lise. She cast a furtive look at Xavier, who seemed taken aback by the bluntness of the duchess's words.

"Forgive me for speaking so freely," Patience said, although there seemed to be not an iota of contrition in her tone. "I fear we have wasted much time seeking a proper match for Lady Elizabeth, and I would rather not do away with more. If there is an interest, the duke and I would see her betrothed sooner rather than later. None of us are growing any younger."

"O-of course, Your Grace," Xavier sputtered, eyeing his father for assistance, but Charlton seemed just as dumbfounded by the sentiment spilling from the duchess's lips. "I-I had only hoped to have some time to know Lady Elizabeth beforehand."

"That is why we are here," Patience reminded him. "That does not discount the fact that we cannot remain here forever waiting on your decision."

Xavier paled, and Lise immediately sensed danger.

Oh, Mother! You are putting far too much pressure on the man!

"I would not mind staying here forever," Lise offered quickly, and all eyes were on her. She cast a warm smile about the table, again locking her gaze with Xavier's becomingly. Her insinuation was not lost on him, and the mild expression of panic began to fade from his face.

"Perhaps, Lady Elizabeth, I could give you a personal tour of the hotel when we have finished our meal?" Xavier asked, and her smile broadened.

"I would enjoy that, Mr. Xavier," she replied.

"Excellent," Patience declared as if they had announced their betrothal. "You two will know one another and conclude this business."

"If I may ask, Your Grace, should these nuptials occur, will your husband be in attendance?" Charlton asked, and Lise's smile fell off her face as though it was made of unsecured wood.

There was something in the proprietor's tone that was rank with wariness, but the unflappable duchess either did not hear it or ignored it.

"Mr. Balfour, I need not tell you the ways of men's work. Certainly, he would not wish to miss the wedding of his only daughter, but if the crown calls—of course, it is duty first."

"Indeed," Charlton murmured.

"Shall we make a toast?" Elias asked, raising his glass, and Lise was grateful for his untimely offer.

"Yes," Xavier agreed, clearly eager to be rid of the smothering tension about them. "I would like to toast Her Grace and the enchanting Lady Elizabeth. May our friendship be long and fruitful."

"Hear, hear," the others chanted, nodding in approval as the glasses clinked.

Lise watched Xavier through her peripheral vision, and he did the same. With trembling hands, she pressed the crystal wine goblet to her lips and permitted the sweetness to warm her belly.

It may not be a long friendship, she thought. *But I am sure I will find it fruitful.*

CHAPTER FOUR

The midday meal seemed to linger on for hours, the tantalizing idea of escorting Elizabeth through the halls of the hotel causing Xavier to lose focus on anything else.

He could plainly see that she was just as captivated by him as he was by her.

At long last, the plates were cleared, and Xavier could barely contain himself from rising as he nodded toward Elizabeth with his arm outstretched.

"Will you allow me a tour?" he asked again, and she blushed against the fabric of her silk gown bewitchingly.

"Yes, of course," she murmured, rising from the chair as young Joshua held it for her.

"Mother, will you escort me?" Elizabeth asked, but the duchess shook her head.

"No, my dear. Take a handmaiden."

Elizabeth seemed surprised but also pleased, and she stepped toward Xavier as a servant hurried after them at a comfortable distance.

"Thank you for such pleasant company," Elizabeth told his family, the gentlemen rising to see her off. "I look forward to spending more time with you."

"The gratitude is ours, Lady Elizabeth," Charlton assured her and bowed. "I hope you will find all you seek here."

"She will," Xavier replied, surprising even himself with the bold statement. He held out his arm for her to take, and she accepted it graciously.

"I will spare you the staff quarters," Xavier chuckled. "I imagine there is nothing there that appeals to you."

"I am certain they are lovely," Elizabeth answered, smiling. "But I would not wish to interrupt the work of the servants."

"My sister spends a great deal of time on the subfloor with the employees."

"You do not sound impressed by her altruism."

"It is not altruism," he grunted. "She thinks of them as our equals."

A delicate eyebrow rose.

"Is that so?"

Xavier went on quickly, sensing disapproval.

"You must understand," he rushed onward, "we have known much of the staff since infancy. Their fathers served us and their father's father."

"I do understand," Elizabeth replied with pensiveness. "There is a staff of over two hundred at Pinehaven. I, too, know the feeling of kinship among the servants and their children. I am simply stunned to learn that others share my feelings. I know no other noblewomen who enjoy the company of their underlings."

"Pinehaven?"

"Our manor house," she said quickly. "Forgive me, I forget you have not been."

"I hope I will one day," Xavier told her. "If only to see a manor house of such splendor."

He felt her arm tense against his, and for barely a second, she seemed to pause in the lobby.

"It is no larger than this hotel," she replied lightly. "I am certain you would be disappointed."

Xavier turned to face her squarely, and she was surprised by his direct stare.

"I daresay, Lady Elizabeth, I have known you for mere hours, and I find it difficult to believe that anything about you could be disappointing."

Again, her cheeks stained with embarrassment, and she shot her sooty eyes away, but Xavier was enraptured with her beauty.

"Shall we continue?" she murmured, glancing about at the milling guests and staff.

"Of course," he said, his tone mildly apologetic. He had not meant to stare at her with such intensity, but he was drawn to her face like a bee to pollen.

She is the daughter of a Duke. I cannot openly gape at her, regardless of how difficult it is to resist.

"Mrs. Compton is kind," Elizabeth offered. "I am unsurprised that she shows compassion for the servants."

"She married one," Xavier barked with unexpected sharpness, and she looked at him in surprise.

"Mr. Compton was a servant?" she asked in shock, again pausing from their walk. "A servant who owns part of the hotel?"

"It is truly a long tale," Xavier muttered, furious with himself for bringing up family history with a near stranger.

She does not feel like a stranger to me. She feels warm and comfortable, as if I have known her before.

"I would very much like to hear it," Elizabeth insisted, but Xavier shook his head and led her up the staircase.

"Truly, I should not have said a word."

"I would not betray your confidence, Mr. Xavier, if you should wish to discuss private matters with me."

Once more, Xavier was struck by her plaintive sweetness, and he longed to blurt out what troubled him about Elias Compton.

If I tell her my fears, she will know I have only asked for this marriage to enhance my hold on this hotel.

He knew that was a trivial fear to have. After all, she was sure to understand that their nuptials would be nothing but an arrangement, one which would benefit both the duke and the Balfours, but suddenly, he did not wish for Elizabeth to consider their union one of business.

"Perhaps we will save such a discussion for another time," he told her when he realized she still stared at him, awaiting an answer.

Inexplicably, a look of sadness crossed over her face.

"I look forward to hearing it, Mr. Xavier."

Silently, he led her onto the second floor, pausing to point out the various art that his mother had chosen with care once upon a time.

"She has quite an eye, your mother," Elizabeth commented appreciatively. "I have always been quite fond of paintings, but I fear I am somewhat of a philistine in comparison to some of my peers."

"My mother does very little for the hotel now," Xavier said grimly, and again he wondered from where this free tongue had come.

"Due to her poor health?" Elizabeth asked softly, and Xavier cast her a sidelong look. She seemed to understand more about Anne than she said.

"Yes," he said quickly. "Due to her poor health."

"Mothers can be difficult," Elizabeth said quite unexpectedly, and Xavier studied her face with interest. He would never have suspected that the duchess caused any sort of problem with her daughter.

"Some more than others," Xavier conceded, but the conversation made him vaguely uncomfortable as though he was speaking ill of his once much-loved mother. It was difficult to recall the precise point when Anne had gone from socialite to melancholic drunk. Once upon a time, she had been so full of life, a mother and wife whom others aspired to emulate.

Yet that had been so long ago, and no one quite remembered Anne Balfour how she was. Suddenly, she was merely a ghost who flittered in and out of their lives.

It is a miracle she managed to find Lady Elizabeth and in such a short time.

He ushered her along the second floor, to the third and fourth, doing his best to keep his attention on the history of his prided hotel and off Elizabeth's nearness. The lines of her neck were intoxicating him, and he was overcome with a desire to kiss her.

"Each floor caters to a unique style of guest," Xavier explained, the words keeping his mouth from doing the brazenly unthinkable. "The fifth floor is reserved for the family."

Elizabeth seemed stunned.

"Our suite is on the fifth floor," she said, and he nodded.

"I hope that you will soon be family," he replied gruffly.

"A-are you...?" she could not finish her thought as though it was unbelievable to her that he might entertain their marriage.

"Proposing?" he asked dryly and she nodded. "I daresay that I best ask your mother first."

"I doubt she will give you any objections in the matter."

They smiled at one another and continued back through the winding halls of the fifth floor to the staircase, bringing them back to where they started.

"I should return to my mother with the news," Elizabeth told him gently. "Should you not do the same with your own family?"

"Indeed," Xavier agreed. "Will you join us for supper?"

"Of course, Mr. Xavier."

"My lady."

He bowed stiffly as she hurried back into the dining room, in search of her mother, and Xavier turned toward the office.

"Is my father inside, Matthew?" he asked, and the concierge nodded but cast Xavier a sly smile.

"Yes, Mr. Xavier. He told me to send you in upon your return."

The statement bothered Xavier.

It is just as much my office as it is Father's—and Elias's. I should not need to announce myself when I come and go.

But he would not permit the annoyance to fester, not when he had such important news. Xavier strode toward the door and entered, speaking without preamble.

"Father, I have wonderful—" his statement died on his lips as he realized that Charlton was not alone in the office. Xavier's smile faded to a deep frown.

"Father, may I speak with you in private?" he demanded, looking pointedly at Elias.

"If this is regarding your engagement, Xavier, I would rather Elias remain," Charlton replied.

"For what purpose? He has no part in this matter!"

"We are concerned, Xavier," Elias offered. "Charlton and I both."

"About what?"

"Lady Elizabeth. Something seems rank," Elias explained. "Can you not sense it?"

Xavier's eyes widened in disbelief.

"That is quite rich coming from you!" he spat indignantly. "You came here under false pretenses and ended up married to the heiress of a profitable hotel!"

"Xavier, mind your tongue!" Charlton barked, but Elias was not one to permit such a slight go unanswered.

"I saved this hotel, Xavier, or have you forgotten?"

"How can I forget? Your presence is a constant reminder of how my father permitted such a thing to occur."

"That is quite enough!" Charlton's face was scarlet with ire, and he rose to his feet, resting the full weight of his body onto his closed knuckles.

"Is it enough?" Xavier snapped. "He is accusing my fiancée of being what? Baggage?"

"I accused Lady Elizabeth of nothing," Elias said flatly. "And you have proposed then?"

"That was what I had come to announce. I did not realize I would be entering a stadium for the battle."

"Xavier, no one is battling you," Charlton growled. "But I daresay before you wed the lady, you must do your due diligence."

"On a duke's daughter?" Xavier scoffed. "What is it you fear? That she is an imposter? She and her mother both?"

The idea was laughable, yet there was an unmistakable graveness in his father's eye.

"I cannot say what it is that troubles us, but there is something amiss, undoubtedly."

"That is hardly an answer, Father. Surely, something caused you to think in such a way."

Charlton frowned and glanced at Elias, their look only causing more anger to spark through Xavier's blood.

Elias will see me displaced in my own house, before my own eyes. I will not have it.

"Well?" Xavier barked. "I demand an answer if you have brought this forth!"

"There is something elusive about the way the duchess takes questions, as though she does not truly have an answer," Elias offered, and Xavier scoffed.

"You will need to do better than that if you wish to protest my marriage!"

"I will not stand in your way if you choose to wed Lady Elizabeth, but I urge you to be wise in the matter," Charlton interjected before Elias could speak again.

"It is a pity you did not urge Emmeline to do the same," Xavier retorted, spinning to leave the office. He had heard quite enough of the foolishness that enshrouded him.

"Xavier!" his father yelled. "The matter is not closed!"

But he was already gone, mounting the stairs toward his mother's bedchambers.

Ridiculous. Mother went to the duchy and met with them in their manor house. There is nothing untoward occurring, regardless of what they might think. Elias is simply laying the ground for his own plans to overtake the hotel. He is attempting to sabotage my happiness.

On the fifth floor, he paused, sinking against the wall with a pounding heart.

That is all it is—jealousy. Elias is plagued with worry about my marriage.

He wondered then, why he rapped on his mother's door and eventually let himself inside to stare at his mother's sleeping figure in her bed.

The smell of liquor permeated the room, and Xavier stared down at Anne worriedly.

His mother was most certainly a drunk, but was she truly melancholic? He could not fathom that she would purposely arrange for him to marry someone who intended him harm, but if she was not in her right mind...

Xavier gritted his teeth furiously and stormed from Anne's bedchambers.

I will not allow Elias Compton this victory, too. Lady Elizabeth and I will marry, and we will do it quickly.

He could hardly wait to see the expression on Elias's face when he heard he had not won this fight.

I will marry Lady Elizabeth within the month, and we will begin trying for a son at once.

CHAPTER FIVE

"I think it is a wonderful idea," the duchess announced. "I will see to all the preparations."

"A month!" Lise choked. "Mother, I never expected for such a short engagement."

The moment she spoke the words, Lise wished she could retract them, the look on Patience's face stern.

"Time is not a luxury we can afford," the duchess reminded her daughter, and Lise nodded, swallowing the stone forming in her throat. "I can only keep your father at bay for so long, Lise."

"Of course," Lise murmured. "Forgive me, Mother. This is all so sudden. I simply have not had the opportunity to process."

"You are fortunate, Lise. You were granted the chance to meet your betrothed beforehand."

The bitterness in Patience's voice was unmistakable, and Lise was consumed with guilt.

You must remember why you are doing this.

"It was his idea," Patience continued. "Clearly, Mr. Xavier is in a rush of his own to wed."

"Yes."

Lise held back the rest of her thoughts and instead focused on what was to come.

"I will need to return to Holden before your father grows suspicious. I will tell him you are in Wales with your aunt."

"You cannot leave me here alone!" Lise gasped. It would be her first time away from the duchy without her family.

"The servants will remain, and you have the Balfours."

"But Mother!"

"You must not cause a fuss, Elizabeth. We have planned this for a long while, even if you never believed it would come to fruition. Perhaps matters are moving along too quickly for you, but I cannot see this through with enough speed. A month seems an eternity in my life."

Shame and compassion touched Lise, but she realized then that it was less being alone in Luton that worried her and more that Patience would return to the duchy without the benefit of her protection.

"Mother, what if Father learns what we are doing?" Lise asked gravely.

"It is my task to ensure he does not."

"But if he does—Mother, we should not part ways."

"It is the only way it will work, Lise. The duke will hardly permit us both to be away for such a long time."

"Mother, what if—"

"Elizabeth, you must heed me now. Your concerns in Holden are finished. You must remain in Luton, and we will reunite in time for the wedding."

Lise eyed her with large, tear-filled eyes.

"Mother, what if you do not return?" she asked quietly. "This will have all been for naught."

"You must not think that way," the duchess told her sternly, but it was clear that Lise's words only echoed her own thoughts. "You must only look to the future."

Misery enveloped Lise as her mother patted her cheek gently.

"All will be well, Elizabeth," she promised. "You maintain matters here, and we will prevail."

There was little else that Lise could do but concede, despite the heaviness weighing on her chest.

"How will you manage the wedding arrangements, Mother?" Lise asked, a last attempt to have her mother reconsider what she was doing.

"Oddly, Mrs. Balfour came to discuss the matter with me. I have agreed to work with her through page."

Lise's head cocked to the side like a perplexed hound.

"That seems tedious," she muttered. "Would it not be sounder to meet?"

"It is the way she prefers it," Patience explained. "And I must confess, I am learning to appreciate her reclusiveness. There is a peace at being left alone. Perhaps I will have an opportunity to experience it for myself one day."

Impulsively, Lise reached forward to squeeze her mother's hand.

"I swear to you, Mother, I will do precisely what it is I need to do to get us away from father," she breathed. "But you must promise to err on the side of caution. You cannot provoke him. You must make yourself scarce when he is about."

"You know it is much easier said than done, child," Patience chuckled, but there was no mirth in the sound.

"Please," Lise begged, tears pooling in her eyes. "You must give me some sense of peace in sending you back to Holden."

"I will call upon your brother," she said, and Lise exhaled with relief. She knew that the duke was much less apt to beat upon them when the marquis was present.

Albeit that is no guarantee.

"What if he cannot come? He is just barely married himself."

"I will implore him," Patience said firmly, gripping Lise's hand. "You must have faith that we will prevail."

Lise wished she shared her mother's confidence, but it was difficult to muster even a small smile, particularly when she knew that she would be in relative safety while her mother was forced to bear the brunt of her father's wicked hand on her own.

How many years did she live this nightmare? Twenty? Twenty-five? Did

Father begin to hit her from the moment of their union, or did he bide his time,
gain her trust?

Lise recalled the first time the duke had ever struck her. She had
been barely five years old. Before that world-shattering moment, Lise
had believed she was the apple of her father's eye, the little lady he
adored.

Oh, how she missed him when he was gone, and she would count
the days until his return.

He must have been whipping Mother before that. I simply did not recall
because he doted on me so much.

If Lise closed her eyes, she could sometimes feel the sting of that
first blow to her small face and hear the sickening impact it made upon
her for years to come. There were more beatings, of course, but it
seemed that none hurt as much as that first one, even when she was
bloodied and bruised, left in the care of an abigail to be mended, only
to be beaten again.

Once, she had been so happy to see the duke returning to the
manor, but she quickly learned to hide away when his carriage neared.

Her mother was never as fortunate. Patience was required at her
husband's side and therefore oft within reach of his tireless fist.

Several times, Patience had been brought back from the brink of
death, but with each revival, more of her spirit was chipped away until
she was merely the Duchess of Holden without anything left inside.

James, the Marquis of Holden, had also endured his share of the
duke's lava-hot temper, but Lise's father seemed to reserve the brunt of
his anger for Patience and Lise.

There had been no doubt in Lise's mind that she or her mother
would inevitably die at the hands of the duke, but what could they do
but endure it?

"If James will not come, you will send for me by messenger," Lise
told her mother firmly. "I will not rest until I know you are in his care.
Or perhaps you should go to Whittaker to be near him."

"You will stop fretting," Patience insisted. "In a short while, we will
be free of this oppression and begin a new life."

If I do what is expected of me.

"Lise?"

"Yes, Mother?"

"You may change your mind at any point, and I will not fault you."

"I will not, Mother. You need not suggest it."

A knock on the door interrupted their conversation, and both women started at the sound.

"Who is there?"

"Chamber service, Your Grace."

Lise arched an eyebrow.

"I did not send for any service," Patience muttered, gliding toward the door. When she opened it, a young man pushed a silver cart through, a smile on his boyish face.

"Mr. Xavier Balfour sends strawberries and champagne, Your Grace, my lady."

"Strawberries?" The women were flabbergasted. "Where in God's name did you find such a thing in the dead of winter?"

"At the Balfour Hotel, Your Grace, all is possible."

He reached for the bottle of wine to pour, and Lise felt a shiver of warmth slide through her.

"He is quite a romantic, is he not?" Patience muttered as the waiter placed the glasses before them.

"If you do not mind me speaking out of school, Your Grace, Xavier Balfour is a fine gentleman. I am pleased to hear of your impending nuptials."

The duchess eyed him.

"You know the Balfours well?" she asked slowly and he nodded.

"I was born here at the hotel."

"What is your name?"

"Joshua. Joshua Milner, Your Grace."

"Very well. That will do, Joshua."

"Very well, Your Grace."

Joshua shot Lise one last smile and disappeared from the sitting room, into the hotel hallway.

"Strawberries in February," the duchess mused. "I daresay your fiancé is attempting to woo you."

"He is merely ensuring we are comfortable," Lise mumbled, reaching for a piece of fruit. It was shockingly sweet, and the succulence only enhanced the feeling of pleasure already coursing through her body.

"Xavier is a difficult man to read," Patience sighed. "I have seen the way he stares at you. He is clearly smitten with your loveliness, but this rush to marriage concerns me."

"Concerns you?" Lise repeated. "We only just spoke of this!"

The duchess shook her head.

"It works to our advantage, Lise, but I have to wonder why."

"Mother, my heart is aflutter with worry. I cannot afford to consider why he wishes to move the date along."

"It does not much matter," Patience assured her. "You will only be wed long enough to gain his trust and gain access to the safe in his office. You must be diligent, Lise. Do not take too much and ensure you are never caught. Work only at night. Soon, we will have enough money to leave the south of England and start a life where no one will know from what we run."

"I remember what I must do, Mother," she sighed. "I have not lost sight of our purpose."

Patience offered her a small smile and nodded.

"Drink your champagne now, child. This is the last time we will be together before your wedding. I cannot bear to be parted with you with a heavy heart."

Reluctantly, Lise accepted a glass and toasted her mother softly.

"To a hopeful future, Elizabeth."

"Indeed."

Their glasses clinked, and both ladies sipped the long-stemmed goblets to take hearty sips.

"Lise?"

"Yes, Mother?"

"Do not make the same mistake I did," she murmured. Lise blinked uncomprehendingly at her mother.

"Do not fall in love with Xavier Balfour. It will only end in heartache for all of us, regardless of how matters result."

Lise tried to scoff, but the scorn did not quite meet her eyes, and her pulse quickened at the warning.

"Love is the last notion I have, Mother."

"That is always when it gets you, darling."

Consternation filled Lise's gut.

"You do not love the duke, after all he has done to you!" she gasped, aghast at the idea.

Patience looked at her sadly.

"Of course, I do," she murmured. "He is the father of my children, the man who has provided for me."

"Mother! He is a brute, a monster!"

"Love is complicated, Elizabeth," she sighed. "That is why I would never wish it upon anyone."

The sage words resonated inside Lise's mind, but they were accompanied by dread as she peered at the strawberries sitting innocently in a pottered bowl, waiting to be tasted.

I will not permit myself to love him, she vowed, stifling the doubt that bubbled in her chest.

CHAPTER SIX

It was impossible not to grow increasingly infatuated with the witty lady who had become a part of Xavier's life in the most inconspicuous way.

The duchess had returned to Holden, leaving Elizabeth heartbroken for days following. She put on a brave face, but it was clear to Xavier that her mother's absence caused a hole in his fiancée's heart.

"In mere weeks, she will return," he told her as they met for breakfast one icy morning close to the eve of St. Valentine's Day. Her mother had been gone for ten days. "You must not fret."

"Forgive me if I seem dismal," Elizabeth apologized. "It is the first time I have been away from home for such an extended period. Perhaps I have a touch of homesickness."

"But this is your home now," Xavier reminded her gently. "I hope you will come to think of it as such."

Her face paled, and she stared at him imploringly.

"You must think me horrid," she gasped. "Of course, this is my home."

There was much to see in the depth of her expressive eyes, but Xavier was uncertain he understood half of what went on behind the veiled irises.

"It is my duty, as your fiancé, to distract you from any unpleasantness until the day of our wedding."

She managed a soft smile.

"You have been most kind, Mr. Xavier, you and your family. Your sister has been the most charming companion. Her child is precious."

Xavier smiled and leaned across the table, his eyes twinkling.

"Is it blasphemous to say I believe ours would be more so?"

The fork in Elizabeth's hand clattered to the table, chipping off a piece of the porcelain plate before her.

"Oh!" she gasped, startled at her reaction. "Forgive me."

She jumped to her feet as Michael appeared at the table to help her rise from the chair.

"No trouble, my lady. I will fetch you another plate at once."

"Do come and sit at my side until they clean the mess, Lady Elizabeth," Xavier instructed, and she gazed at him uncertainly.

"Of course," she mumbled when he met her gaze in confusion. Michael reappeared to handle her chair, and Elizabeth sank to his side, her face nearly opaque.

"Are you unwell?" Xavier asked, peering at her.

"I am fine," she replied. "I merely startled myself."

"Did my talk of children alarm you?" Xavier asked, his heart beginning to pump.

Perhaps she does not like children.

He found that difficult to believe. Over the past week, he had seen how well she had handled baby Catherine, and the infant had taken to her easily. It was clear to see that Elizabeth had a natural mothering way about her.

"No," she replied quickly. "Of course not."

She smiled at him but it did not quite meet her eyes although when he peered more closely, he also noted a deep sadness that he had not seen before.

I wonder what secrets she hides.

Xavier vowed to learn them all.

———

Perhaps God had heard his silent prayer for when Xavier woke on St. Valentine's Day morning, a gentle blanket of snow had graced the countryside around the hotel. He could not have been more pleased with the weather, and he hurried to dress quickly.

He brushed aside his manservant.

"Not today, Nicholas. I will dress myself."

"As you wish, Mr. Xavier."

"Will you send word to Lady Elizabeth that I would like to see her in the office at eight o'clock?"

"Yes, Mr. Xavier."

Nicholas exited his chambers to deliver the message, and Xavier opened a drawer to withdraw the valentine he had made especially for his betrothed. He had impressed himself with the intricate detail, the fine embroidery and lace trim. Arts were hardly Xavier's forte, but somehow, he had created something beautiful for the comely lady who would soon be his wife.

In less than a fortnight, a major change had occurred in Xavier, one that he not only felt but that others had noticed.

"I daresay, I have never seen you smile so much," Emmeline told him. "You are smitten with Lady Elizabeth!"

"She is my fiancée," Xavier replied lightly, but Emmeline chuckled.

"Marriage and love are not mutually exclusive," she reminded him as if he needed to be told.

There was a rap on the door of his bedchambers.

"Come."

"Good morrow, Mr. Xavier."

He whirled at the sound of Elizabeth's voice, and for a moment he thought he was imagining her presence in his quarters.

"Good morrow, my lady. Are you well?"

She lowered her eyes, her gaze falling to the pleated skirts of her gown before she looked up again.

"I must speak with you about a private matter," she murmured, and fear gripped his heart.

"Of course," he said, looking about for her chaperone, but stunningly, she was alone.

"My abigail waits in the hall," she assured him and he exhaled, with disappointment.

For shame, he chided himself. *Ladies do not enter the bedchambers of their betrothed unattended.*

"I must return to Holden," Elizabeth blurted out, and shock caused him to reel back as if her words had given him a physical blow.

"W-why?" he demanded, struggling to keep his voice steady. "Have you changed your mind about this union?"

Her eyes widened, and she shook her head.

"Oh! Certainly not!" she promised, realizing that her statement had caused him distress.

"My word, Mr. Xavier. I do cause you a great deal of distress with my words, do I not?"

"Only when I misunderstand them," Xavier quipped. His brow furrowed.

"Why must you return to Holden? Has someone sent word?"

"No," Elizabeth replied quietly. "That is precisely the point. I have not heard from my mother since she left."

Relief colored his face.

"Her Grace is quite well," he assured her, but he was shaking his head as he said it. "She met with my mother only yesterday."

"She what?" Elizabeth demanded, her face gaunt with shock. "Are you quite certain?"

"I am," he replied, closing the short space between them and took her hand softly. "It was the queerest thing. My mother never takes visitors, yet they were having tea in her suite as though they were companions from childhood."

"Here?"

"Indeed. I am bewildered that she did not call on you while she was here," he continued. "Perhaps she tried?"

"Perhaps..."

There was doubt and confusion in Elizabeth's voice.

"If you wish, I can send a messenger to her—"

"No!" Elizabeth interjected quickly. "I mean, there is no need. I will see her when she becomes available. The life of a duchess is quite complicated."

"I imagine that is so. You should consider yourself fortunate that you are marrying a lowly commoner."

He grinned and her worried face broke into a wan smile.

"I would not call the heir to a hotel such as this a lowly commoner," she laughed. "However, you do make a decent point—I would not wish to live the life of a high-end nobleman."

"Will you join me in the office? I have a wonderful day planned for us both."

Her brows raised slightly.

"The office?"

"Indeed. I must take a stop at the safe. Will you come?"

"The safe? Uh...yes, of course," Elizabeth agreed. "Shall we go now?"

"One moment."

Xavier hurried back to the bedchamber and reached for the valentine card he had made for her before rejoining her.

"Happy St. Valentine's Day," he told her, handing her the paper. Her eyes grew large and she gasped, a gloved hand covering her mouth with embarrassment.

"I did not get you anything!" she muttered.

"I do not expect anything but your company today," he replied, unhurt that she had forgotten. The days since her mother left had been difficult on her. He doubted very much that she had noticed the date at all.

Slowly, she opened the card with shining eyes and read the sweet poem he had struggled so hard to write. It had taken him hours, and even so, he was not sure it depicted the feelings he was hoping to portray.

"Oh, Mr. Xavier," she murmured. "It is beautiful. Thank you. I have never received a gift for St. Valentine's Day before."

Their eyes met, and he could read the excess of emotion in her face.

"This is merely the beginning, my dear."

He leaned in closer, his breath catching across her cheek.

"Perhaps, one day," he breathed, "you will think to call me Xavy when we are alone?"

She tilted her head and smiled.

"Perhaps," she jested. "One day."

"Come along then, my lady. Let us go to the office, and then I have a carriage ride waiting for us outside."

"A carriage ride? To where?"

"Does it much matter? It is a winter wonderland outside, and we have all the day to enjoy it."

With arms entwined, they found their way to the lobby and entered the office under Matthew's watchful eye.

"My father is gone to Cambridge, is he not?" Xavier asked the concierge.

"He is, Mr. Xavier, but Mr. Compton is about if you need him."

An expression of fury fell on Xavier's face.

"Pray tell," he growled. "What could Mr. Compton possibly tell me that I do not already know?"

Matthew balked.

"Yes, Mr. Xavier."

Elizabeth squeezed his arm gently as they moved inside the vast room.

"You were quite brusque with him, were you not?" Elizabeth asked gently. "He only meant to be helpful."

Xavier scowled and look at her.

"It is not Matthew who infuriates me. It is Elias Compton. He walks about as though he owns the entire hotel."

"Does he? I had not noticed that."

Xavier dropped to his knees and removed a key from the pocket of his waistcoat before turning to the safe and unlocking the heavy leaden door.

"It is nothing specific," he conceded. "But I know what he wants."

"What would that be?"

"He intends to overtake the hotel one day. He started by marrying Emmeline, and soon he will have a gaggle of children running amok, claiming their grandfather's stake."

He clamped his mouth closed as he realized what he had just said, his face waning. Elizabeth was silent, and he slowly turned to look at her through his sidelong vision, a small satchel in his hand.

"Here," he muttered, unsure if she was upset by his revelation or merely pondering his words.

"What is it?"

She stepped toward him to accept the bag, but Xavier had already slipped the contents out into his smooth hand.

A sparkling ruby ring shone up at Elizabeth, and she gaped at it.

"This belonged to my grandmother's grandmother," he explained. "It is one of most treasured heirlooms, and I want you to wear it."

"Oh, I do not know—"

"I am the firstborn, Lady Elizabeth. It is mine to give to my wife, and you will be said wife. Unless, that is, you have changed your mind."

Her eyes sparkled with unshed tears, her gaze traveling from the ring to the card in her hands and finally resting on his face.

"I have not changed my mind." Her voice was barely a whisper, a fusion of sadness and joy.

I may never understand her, but I can see how deeply she feels.

"May I put it on your finger?"

"Y-yes," she mumbled, extending her left hand for him. It did not shock him that the ring fit perfectly as though it had been designed for her hand a hundred years earlier.

"Come along now," he said lightly, willing the tears from falling down her stricken face. "Our carriage awaits us."

She did not respond, but before they departed, he noticed that she paused to cast one last look back into the office.

"Have you forgotten something?"

"No, Xavy," she breathed. "I will remember it all."

CHAPTER SEVEN

Shame clung to Lise like a spiderweb. She was present, yet not fully, in the fortnight leading to the wedding, which was to take place on the first of March. Perhaps because there was no reminder of what she was meant to do in the days following the wedding, Lise permitted herself to appreciate the gentleman who showed her nothing but kindness.

No matter how she tried to remember her mother's prophetic words, she could not help herself from admiring his wonderful qualities or losing herself in the regal lines of his handsome face.

If she had tried to resist Xavier's charms, Lise was sure she would have been unsuccessful. There was never a day that he did not find fresh flowers to leave in her chambers.

Where in God's name is he discovering such luscious plants? She marveled one morning, three days before they were to wed. It was not only the small gifts that he bestowed upon her, of course. His emerald eyes depicted the feelings he felt toward her, and despite his full days of working about the hotel, Xavier seemed to find the time to eat with her and walk along the icy outdoors.

The guilt struck her the worst when she caught a glimpse of the glinting ruby ring upon her finger.

Will the outcome of this scar him from courting again? Will he be able to court again and marry?

Certainly, she had heard of noblemen finding ways through the Church to annul their marriages when their wives went astray, but would the same apply to someone like Xavier Balfour?

There is no one else like Xavier Balfour. He is truly one of a kind.

Despite the affections she was nurturing for the hotel heir, Lise did not forget the ultimate goal—and she had already begun to steal some of the monies put away in the safe.

On the nights when she had supper with Xavier, she would invariably "borrow" the key to the safe and steal away in the middle of the night to the office when she knew the concierge was away.

She had gotten to know the staff on polite terms, more so to learn their routine than for the sake of friendship.

I have no business making alliances with anyone.

She knew that the concierge walked the hotel between the hour of two and half past the hour, which was when she would steal inside the office and withdraw a few dollars to add to her and her mother's escape fund.

In the morning, she would simply slip the key back into Xavier's waistcoat, and he was none the wiser.

It was becoming increasingly difficult to shift herself between the lady who wanted to save herself from a perilous life and the one who was falling in love with her fiancé.

No! She told herself sharply. *There was never a plan to fall in love. Xavier has reasons of his own for wooing you so strongly. You must not fall into a trap, believing his motives are any purer than yours.*

Sighing, Lise moved toward the armoire, glancing back at the door to ensure her abigail had not re-entered the room. Carefully, she counted the growing pile of notes, which she had hidden carefully among the special pearls she wore only on the most important of occasions.

Perhaps I will wear them at my wedding.

Mary did return to the suite then, and Lise hastily put aside her ill-gotten gains, stifling the moan of disappointment in herself and the situation.

It was both a blessing and a curse that her mother had not shown herself once since returning to Holden. Lise was certain that Patience had stayed away to ensure that the matter was not more difficult for her daughter. It had taken a long while for the hollow pain of her departure to ease from Lise's gut. She was certain her mother had remained away to spare her more discontent.

Xavier helped me through that time.

"My lady, shall I help you dress?" Mary asked and Lise realized she had fallen off into a slight reverie.

"Yes," Lise replied, turning away from the wardrobe to stand before the mirror. Mary wriggled the corset over her undergarments and cinched it tightly around her full bosom before selecting a simple but elegant dress of velvet and lace. The periwinkle was a flattering color for Lise's fair complexion, and when Mary began to do her hair up, Lise stopped her.

"Leave it down," she instructed. "Mr. Xavier prefers it that way."

"As you wish, my lady."

A blush of embarrassment and worry sprang to Lise's cheeks. She tried to tell herself that it did not matter what Xavier preferred, that he was merely a means to an end, but that lie no longer had a semblance of truth in her own ears.

Why can I not enjoy our time together? She thought defensively as though her own mind was another person arguing her inconsistent emotions. *Must I walk about in a cloud of gloom?*

"Lady Elizabeth, Mr. Xavier fears he will be unable to join you for breakfast," Mary told her and Lise whirled around, startling the servant.

"How is that?"

"I am told he has business in Luton today."

Without a word, Lise brushed by her handmaid and rushed into the corridor, her heart thumping with fear.

"Lady Elizabeth!" Mary called after her, following close on her heels, but Lise barely acknowledged her as she knocked on Xavier's door.

"My lady, he is already gone. He left early this morning, but he did not wish to wake you. He will return this evening."

Lise was the color of fresh cream when she turned away from the door.

"I wish you had woken me," she murmured, and Mary lowered her eyes.

"Forgive me, my lady."

There was nothing to be done about it now, and Lise shuffled back toward her chambers, her pulse still racing.

In her hand, she clutched the safe key, which was to be returned to her fiancé. Now, she was faced with a dilemma.

Should she hold onto it until he returned or leave it somewhere conspicuous, leading him to believe he had lost it?"

For all she knew, he had already attempted to use the safe that very morning. If she simply slipped it back into his pocket upon his return, he would know something was amiss.

Yet if I drop it near the office, he will be more apt to keep an eye on it.

"Lady Elizabeth, is there a matter?" Mary asked, staring at her with large eyes.

"No," Lise muttered. "I am merely disappointed that I will not dine with him this morrow. I had grown quite accustomed to our morning meals."

Lise did not miss the swoon in Mary's eyes.

"I do hope to find a man who adores me as Mr. Xavier adores you, my lady," Mary murmured, and more shame flushed through Lise.

Good Lord, what am I doing? I cannot continue like this!

"Mr. and Mrs. Compton await you in the dining room," Mary offered timidly, misconstruing Lise's expression as annoyance.

"Very well," Lise sighed. She was not particularly in the mood to see anyone at that moment, but she could not hole herself away in Xavier's absence. There was still a role to be played.

She finished dressing fully, permitting Mary to pinch her cheeks for a modicum of blush and made her way to the dining room with the abigail escorting her.

"Good morrow, Lady Elizabeth," Elias called as she arrived, rising from his chair.

"Good morrow," Lise replied, nodding as she was seated. The young waiter, Joshua tended to the family.

"I trust you slept well despite that ice storm," Emmeline said, and Lise looked toward her in confusion.

"Ice storm?" she echoed, realizing she had not bothered to look outside a window yet that morning.

"My word!" Emmeline chuckled. "Perhaps we should change suites! We were up all night."

"Catherine had much to say about it," Elias agreed, seeming surprised. "She cried all night long. You heard nothing?"

"Not a stir in the night," Lise replied, glancing toward the windows. To her utter amazement, the outdoors appeared encased in glass beyond the panes. A pang of concern fluttered through her.

"It is hardly a safe day for travel," she murmured. "The horses do not handle ice well."

"Your betrothed will return to you safely, my lady," Emmeline assured her, smiling kindly. "Unfortunately, however, you are left in our company for the day."

Lise managed a smile despite her increasing worry. The sun had not shone through the intense gray clouds, indicating that perhaps more bad weather was on the way.

"I can think of no better way to spend the day," Lise replied. She could not help but notice that Elias studied her with particular scrutiny.

"Will Her Grace be arriving soon?" he asked, and Lise turned her attention toward him fully.

"Certainly," she replied. "For the wedding on Friday, of course."

"And the duke?"

It was the first time anyone had questioned her directly about her father, and Lise was temporarily taken aback by the pointedness.

"I-I cannot say," she replied evasively.

"The duchess did not mention it?" Elias pressed, and Lise eyed him warily. His queries were far too direct for casual conversation, but to her relief, Emmeline prevented her from answering.

"Darling, I daresay that these are questions you should save for the duchess. She and Mother are responsible for the preparations."

Lise gave Emmeline a grateful look, but Elias seemed discontent with the response.

"Of course," he muttered, but Lise sensed that the matter was far from over.

"Joshua," Emmeline called, "we will have our tea now."

"How is the baby?" Lise asked, eager to lift the slight tension over the table. "She is growing before my eyes."

"Indeed," Emmeline chuckled. "I have only just learned to leave her in the care of the nanny, but there is much work to be done in the hotel."

"What is it you do about the hotel, Mrs. Compton?" Lise asked, the curiosity getting the best of her. She had no doubt that there were endless tasks to be accomplished, but Emmeline's role was elusive.

Emmeline looked to her in surprise.

"If you wish, I can take you about with me and give you a feel for what you, too, will find yourself doing once you are Lady Elizabeth Balfour."

A chill shot through Lise's body, although she was unsure which aspect caused her the most unease.

"Oh," Lise laughed nervously. "Clearly, I will have little part of the daily operations."

"Why is that?" Elias' brow raised, and again, Lise was plagued by the sense he was watching her with far too much interest.

It is your own guilty conscience that makes you believe that.

"She is a lady, Eli, not a hostess," Emmeline chided gently. She offered Lise a warm smile.

"It is not that!" Lise protested, embarrassed that the Comptons thought her spoiled. "I only meant that you already have your defined roles within the hotel. I certainly would not wish to intrude on your ways, particularly when I know so little about the business."

"You will learn, and there is enough work for everyone," Emmeline laughed. "Is that not so, Eli?"

"Indeed!" Elias said with enthusiasm, which surprised Lise. She would not have expected a man who wished to take over the hotel to allow insiders into his affairs. Yet he seemed relieved that there might be another set of hands to help them.

"I would prefer that Emmeline rest more," he confided, noting her look. "Her place is with the household, not the business."

"Of course," Emmeline interjected, "that is only until Lady Elizabeth is with a child of her own."

Elias blushed at the words, but Emmeline did not seem to be perturbed by her forward speak in the least.

They are upperclassmen, yet they speak so freely, Lise thought with a twinge of envy. *There is a level of comfort between them that I have never seen in another pair.*

Lise wondered if she and Xavier would ever become so at peace with one another.

No, she thought mournfully. *You will not. You will never have the chance.*

CHAPTER EIGHT

"Lady Elizabeth seems to be adjusting well to our ways," Charlton commented as the coach made its way back toward the hotel from Luton. Occasionally, the cab would lurch precariously as the horses lost their footing against the ice, and the interior was freezing, despite the heavy blankets bestowed upon both father and son.

It was not a long journey back, but it seemed to be taking twice the time as usual because of the dangerous conditions.

"She is," Xavier conceded, a smile touching his face as he thought about his fiancée. Every day he felt that he was growing closer to her, and he found himself looking forward to the upcoming wedding. He had missed her terribly that day. It was the first they had been parted since her arrival almost a month earlier.

"Your mother and the duchess seem to have built an unlikely friendship," Charlton said, and Xavier cast him a stare.

"Have they? I imagine they have found common ground in the wedding preparations."

"Perhaps," Charlton replied in a most evasive way. Xavier's eyes narrowed slightly as he waited for his father to complete whatever it was that was on his mind, but Charlton said nothing else.

They continued homeward in silence for a long while, cringing as they slid along.

"Are you quite certain you wish to marry, Xavier?"

Xavier whirled his head to stare at his father in disbelief.

"I should hope so, Father. The event will occur in three days."

"I would loathe to see you regret a decision made in haste," his father said shortly.

"It is not a decision made in haste, Father. I have grown quite fond of Lady Elizabeth. Perhaps I was propelled into action in hopes of stopping Elias, but I must confess, the match is ideal."

"Do you believe she feels the same?"

Xavier tensed.

"I have no doubt," he said coldly. "And I will not have you or Elias starting with your blasted theories about her intentions. She is a noble, honorable woman, who will make a fine wife."

Again, Charlton fell into quiet, but Xavier continued to stare at him stonily.

"Father, Lady Elizabeth has done nothing to warrant your suspicion. I have spoken with Mother about her peerage, and she is not anyone but who she claims to be."

"I am aware of that," Charlton agreed. "When you refused to investigate the matter, I had my barrister check on your behalf."

Xavier felt a rush of anger surge through his bones.

"You have no right!"

"The matter is done, Xavier. There is nothing to fear on that front. Moreover, the duchess is also who she claims."

"A waste of time and funds," Xavier snarled. "If it is not Elias overtaking our hotel, it is you throwing our money away on trivialities."

"There is still something about Lady Elizabeth that concerns me," Charlton insisted. "I cannot say what it is, but I will not rest easy knowing you have married her."

The statement was blunt and struck Xavier in his heart like a blade.

"I will not terminate the engagement."

"I did not expect that you would," Charlton sighed. "I have seen the eyes you give her, but I must say, Xavier, she does not appear to return your affection."

Xavier had heard enough, and he scowled at his father.

"Pray tell, Father, what is it you believe the lady wants from me, an heir to a hotel? What could she possibly desire?"

"All I can say for certain, Xavier, is that the duchess has brought your mother out of her shell. I see more of Anne now than I have in the past two decades. I wonder if the duchess is filling your mother's head with tales."

Xavier gaped at him, a slow understanding seeping into him.

"Are you envious, Father?"

Charlton scoffed.

"Envious of women?" he snapped. "Are you mad?"

"Envious of the fact that neither Mother nor I am constantly seeking your approval now."

Father and son stared at one another, an identical frown on each of their faces.

"Your mother never sought my approval," Charlton replied quietly. "And you have never needed it, contrary to what you might think."

"You have Elias now," Xavier told him coldly. "You need not worry about my affairs. Focus on your new son."

Charlton's eyes shadowed, and he shook his head slowly.

"You have never understood me," he told his son. "All I have ever done has been for the best of this hotel, for our family."

"Walter Greene?" Xavier retorted caustically. "Was that the best for the family? For the hotel?"

"You are rehashing ancient history to make a point," Charlton snapped. "I am merely expressing my concern as your father."

"You cannot even say what your concern is regarding!"

They continued to hold the other's stare until Charlton finally broke the gaze and hung his head.

"No," he agreed. "I cannot. Call it intuition or a terrible sense of foreboding, but I cannot help but feel that Lady Elizabeth and the duchess are wrought with trouble."

"You are mistaken," Xavier said flatly. "And I do not wish to hear another word on the matter. You said you would not forbid our union. You cannot recant your promise three days before the event."

"I will not," Charlton replied. "Nor would I without proof of my own suspicions, but I had hoped that perhaps you felt the same uncertainty when you were with her."

"I do not."

Xavier turned toward the fogged window and tried to make sense of where they were, but it was far too dark and the frost made visibility difficult.

He was sure they were almost back to the hotel, and for that, Xavier was grateful.

He did not wish to engage in any further conversation with his father even though he could tell Charlton had much more to say.

Elizabeth loves me. I can see it plainly in her face whenever she looks at me. She is as eager to marry me as I am her.

Yet not for the first time, he wondered why.

Why had the duchess agreed to marry her only daughter to an heir of a hotel? Surely, there were much better matches that could be made for a lady of Elizabeth's standing.

And they did agree to a quick marriage also. Why?

Xavier did not smother the grunt of frustration that left his lips, startling his father.

"What is it?"

"What is it?" Xavier echoed. "You have filled my mind with untoward thoughts, ones that would have never entered my mind if you had stayed out of my marriage."

"I am trying to help you, Xavier, not hurt you."

"I came to you for help, if you will recall. You sent me to Mother. Now you have too much to say on the matter."

"I will not speak of it again," Charlton said slowly. "Forget I spoke at all."

"I intend to do precisely that!"

Again, he whipped his head to stare out the window indignantly, and he exhaled with relief. The lights of the hotel appeared, the lanterns lit enchantingly against the crystalline night, and the coach slipped up to the entranceway without incident.

The coachman barely managed to open the door before Xavier scurried out and toward the double doors leading into the lobby.

Before he could place a gloved hand to the handle, it flew inward, and he was staring at Elizabeth's waxen face.

"Oh, thank the Lord!" she gasped.

"What is it?" he demanded, terror seizing him as he stared at her. "What has happened?"

She gaped at him with shock in her eyes.

"You have been gone since before dawn! It is nearing the hour of eight, and the weather is ghastly! You ask what has happened?" she almost shouted. He blinked several times, almost confused by her outburst.

"You were concerned?" he asked in disbelief.

"Naturally, I was concerned!" she choked, but slowly the color seemed to be filling her face, and Elizabeth exhaled.

"Forgive me," she murmured. "I should not have been so shrill about it, but I have been pacing the floors for hours, waiting for you to return."

She reached out her hands for his, and he took them eagerly.

"I am sorry you were so concerned," he told her tenderly. "We had intended to return sooner, but our tasks took much longer than expected."

Through his peripheral vision, Xavier saw his father saunter through the lobby. Charlton's mouth tightened at the corners when his eyes rested on Elizabeth, but he did not pause to speak with either one of them.

You need not be jealous, Father, Xavier thought with some smugness. *Even if Mother could not be bothered to worry if you were alive or dead.*

"Come along," Elizabeth ordered him, tugging at his hand. "You are frozen to your very core, and you will catch your death. I will arrange tea for us in the dining room."

Impulsively, she leaned into him and embraced him quite unexpectedly. He felt a slight tug on his waistcoat, and she withdrew, looking embarrassed.

"I was terribly worried," she repeated, staring at him with an expression of adoration in her eyes.

"If I had known you were beside yourself, my lady, I would have made a better effort to return sooner."

"All is well that ends well," she announced. "Shall we?"

Before leading her into the dining room to warm himself by the hearth with tea, he looked toward the office where his father had disappeared and shook his head slightly.

You see, Father? She loves me. Your fears are unfounded.

————

On the day before the wedding, Xavier noticed the key to the safe was missing from where he always held it in the pocket of his waistcoat. He had it only the evening before but when he went to dress that morning, it was no longer there.

The mystery alarmed him as he retraced his steps back to the office and looked about for signs of the key he had never once misplaced.

It was there that Elizabeth found him, crawling about the floor on his hands and knees.

"My word, Xavier, what are you doing?" she giggled from the doorway.

"Oh!" he gasped, humiliation tinging his face as he jumped to his feet to straighten himself. "I lost something, and I was looking for it."

"We do have servants for such tasks," she reminded him, but Xavier knew he could not tell the staff the significance of the key. They would rob the hotel blind if they chanced upon it.

"Are you all right?" Elizabeth asked, gliding toward him, her skirts rustling gently as she moved. "You seem wan."

"I must find this key," he murmured, looking about the floor from a standing position this time. "I had it just last night."

"A key?" she repeated slowly. Her voice croaked slightly, but Xavier barely noticed in his perplexity.

"Yes," he muttered. "The key to the safe. I keep it in my waistcoat...where could the deuced thing be?"

"Oh!" Elizabeth called brightly, hurrying beside the desk. She leaned down and picked up a long, brass instrument. "Is this it?"

Relief washed through Xavier, and he chuckled.

"Indeed it is," he laughed, accepting it from her white glove. "I thought I had looked there before you arrived."

"Perhaps you simply needed fresh eyes," Elizabeth said breathlessly, smiling at him.

"Perhaps I simply need you at my side so that I do not lose my wits, too," he laughed, reaching to pull her hands into his. "Thank you, Lise. I cannot explain the damage that would have done if it had fallen into the wrong hands."

Elizabeth cocked her head back to stare into his face, and for the first time in days, he saw a familiar shadow forming over her face.

"What is the matter, my love?" he asked softly. "Why do you seem forlorn?"

"Do I? Perhaps it is merely nerves. In one day, we will be man and wife."

He raised her hands to his mouth and kissed them gently before lowering their arms.

"I, for one, am looking forward to it even though it does not much seem that a wedding is being prepared, does it?"

He looked over her shoulder into the lobby and shook his head.

"I have yet to see extra staff or décor coming through," he muttered. "It is odd, is it not?"

"I would not know," she replied softly. "I have never been married."

"Ho! Ho!" Xavier chortled. "Yet I am sure you have attended your share of ceremonies. Surely, you must agree that there should be a bustle occurring in preparation for the wedding."

"I have not given anything much thought but breakfast," Elizabeth replied. "Perhaps I am too simplistic."

Xavier looked at her and nodded slowly.

"You are correct. If there is anything amiss with the preparations, certainly our mothers will know of it."

Even if your mother is in absentia and mine is likely ape-drunk at this very moment.

A strange stirring unsettled his stomach.

No one has much discussed the wedding either. I have not received messages of congratulations nor gifts.

The more Xavier thought about it, the more he realized how odd the days leading to their union seemed to him.

He distinctly recalled Emmeline's wedding. It had been an extravagant affair.

Of course, Father had invested his own time and interest. I only have Mother.

Xavier tried to smother his resentment, particularly when Elizabeth stared at him with such plaintiveness.

"Darling, are you all right?" she asked.

"Yes," he replied. "How could I not be when I am about to wed the most intoxicating lady in all of England?"

"How fortunate she must be!"

"I hope she feels so."

"How could a lady in your company feel anything but lucky?" Elizabeth murmured, and Xavier's tall form was painted with warmth.

"Come along, my dear. I would not wish for you to perish from hunger on the morrow before our nuptials."

"That would be quite a tragedy."

"Or a scandal!" Xavier quipped, and Elizabeth cast him a sidelong look as she took his arm.

"We would not wish to scandalize the hotel."

He thought he detected a note of bitterness, but when he studied her face, he saw nothing that indicated displeasure.

We are both fraught with nerves today, he decided. His hand carefully touched the key in his pocket, and he reminded himself to keep a better eye upon it.

It is a blessing that Elizabeth found it when she did. I cannot imagine what Father would have to say about it if it went missing.

"Would you prefer if I hold it for you?" Elizabeth asked, noticing his hand where it remained over his pocket. "I could easily keep it on a chain about my neck."

"You would do that for me?"

"If it puts your mind at ease," she replied, but she did not meet his eyes. "I will rarely be away from your side once we are wed. You need not go far to search for it."

"That is very true," he agreed, withdrawing it from his pocket. "I would not wish to burden you."

"It is no burden," she insisted, taking the key from his hands. "I will have the goldsmith fashion a chain."

"I would prefer that my father know nothing about this," he said and instantly wished he had worded the ask differently. Hurt flashed over her face before she could control it.

"May I ask why?"

Xavier inhaled and shook his head apologetically.

"It is not you," he began but his mind was whirling to think of the right words as he spoke. "He is naturally suspicious of newcomers."

"He is not suspicious of Elias," Elizabeth replied pointedly.

"Elias holds interest in the hotel."

"As do I! I will be your wife!"

Xavier gave her a look, urging her to lower her voice. They were attracting the attention of passersby in the lobby.

"Lise," he offered placatingly, "you simply must earn his trust. He will warm to you as he did to Elias. I assure you, he was not fond of the idea of Elias, either."

She did not respond, but a muscle in her fine jaw twitched slightly.

"Do you understand?"

"Yes," she muttered. "I will say nothing to your father."

"Good. Come along, then."

No sooner had he taken a step did he pause again and look at her.

"Should the duchess not be here already? Surely she will stay the night to be here for the morning?"

"I am sure she will be along," Elizabeth said shortly, but the answer only raised the confusion that Xavier had been manifesting earlier.

There are no preparations being made, no new staff present. The duchess is conspicuously absent, yet Elizabeth is nonchalant about this as though it does not bother her in the least.

He permitted Elizabeth to tug his arm along, the ruffles of her dress falling over the arm of his crisp shirt, but uncertainty was mounting inside him.

Xavier was beginning to question if the wedding was going to occur at all.

CHAPTER NINE

"Mother!"

Lise spun away from the mirror and flew toward the door, almost tripping over her veil in the process. She flung herself into Patience's arms and willed herself not to cry.

Although she had done her best to hide the blotches about her face, it was clear that the duchess had endured an agonizing beating before arriving at the hotel, and Lise choked back a sob as she examined her face.

"Leave us," she instructed the servants who milled about, helping her prepare for the wedding, which was mere moments away.

Without a word or protest, her suite emptied, leaving only the mother and daughter to look at one another.

"What has he done to you?" Lise demanded. "Does he know about our plan?"

"No," Patience assured her. "The duke knows nothing. What of the Balfours? Do they suspect anything?"

Lise dropped her arms and turned away, gathering the mass of lace in her hands as she padded back toward the glass to look at herself.

Truly, she had never been more beautiful in the elegant gown of lace and silk. A crown of white held the heavy veil in place, spilling over her shoulders to enshroud her in a sea of white. This was all a stunning contrast to her ebony hair and stormy, gray eyes, a true vision for even Lise's own gaze to behold.

Instead of answering her mother's question, she posed one of her own.

"Why did you stay away, Mother? I know you visited with Mrs. Balfour. Why did you not come to see me?"

"I needed you to remain focused on winning over Mr. Xavier, darling. I wanted nothing more than to see you, but I could not distract you from our scheme."

"Nothing could!" Lise breathed, her eyes falling again on her mother's bruised face. "Does he know you have come here?"

"Of course not, Lise. You must not worry about your father. He is a concern of the past now...provided you have already begun to collect for our fund."

"I have," Lise replied, hurrying toward the armoire. "I would prefer if you take it. I have the key to the safe now. When the time is right, we will take what we need and be on our way."

Her voice trembled slightly as she spoke the words, and Patience caught it immediately.

"You sound uncertain," the duchess said as Lise pressed the money she had acquired into her mother's hand.

Lise raised her eyes and met her mother's.

"They are good souls," she sighed. "I am hardly of a character to steal from hardworking men."

"It is not something I expect you did with a happy heart," Patience agreed, guilt clouding her own eyes. "If our own lives were not at risk, I would never agree to such criminality. I trust you know that."

"Yes, Mother, of course."

Lise lowered her gaze.

"There is more than that," Patience guessed. "You have developed feelings for Mr. Xavier."

"No!" Lise lied quickly. "I-he is also a good man, but that does not change the fact that we must go."

"Lise, you have not told him of our plans, have you?"

Shocked, Lise shook her head.

"I would never endanger us in such a way!" she cried.

"He will simply call upon your father, and we will be forced back to Pinehaven in chains if need be. Your father will never let us go."

"I know that, Mother!"

And she did know. There would be no fairy story ending for her and Xavier, even if he were to learn the truth and forgive her sins. The moment the duke learned that she had married without his consent, it was precisely as the duchess had said—the marriage would be annulled, and they would be brought back to Holden.

No matter how attached she had become to Xavier, remaining was not an option. It would be a death sentence.

"My lady?" Emmeline knocked gently and looked into the room. "Oh, forgive me, Your Grace. I did not realize you had come."

"I have only just arrived," Patience replied.

"The ceremony is about to commence. Shall I inform the priest that you are ready, Lady Elizabeth?"

Lise looked to her mother and quickly blinked back the tears forming in her eyes.

"Yes," Lise muttered. "I am ready."

———

There was a look of deep suspicion on Xavier's face, which sent chills through Lise's body.

"Mother, where is everybody?" she whispered, immediately understanding his expression. "There are barely twenty guests."

"That is for the best," her mother insisted, squeezing her arm. "Hush now. Your groom is staring."

The duchess fell away to take her spot among the guests, leaving Lise to walk alone across the aisle, the dread in her gut mounting.

This should not be so difficult. You are to wed the man you desire, a good man, one who loves you undoubtedly, and yet...

Yet it was all a farce, a sham.

Lise clamped her mouth closed and proceeded down the aisle toward the altar where the priest waited with Xavier. Slowly, the look of distrust melted away from Xavier's face when his eyes rested on her approaching form, but Lise was having a difficult time returning his steadfast stare.

Suddenly, the air was stiflingly hot, and she wanted to dart from the chapel and gulp back huge breaths of clean air, but somehow, she managed to make her way toward her bridegroom.

She was grateful that the veil covered the panic on her face until she was at Xavier's side and he lifted it to study her eyes.

"Kneel," the priest instructed, and Xavier cast her a warm beam to reassure her before helping her to the altar where they lowered their heads in prayer.

Father Callaway droned on, but Lise did not hear a word, her eyes darting toward the few people in the pews.

Charlton Balfour sat at his wife's side as though they were strangers to one another. To the left of Mrs. Balfour sat Emmeline and Elias, the baby asleep in the nanny's arms at the side of the pew.

Several other servants were in attendance, including the head housekeeper, Antoinette, and the maître d', but there was not another familiar face among them.

Of course, Lise realized. *We cannot invite those whom we know of, or the word will get back to Father before we have a chance to escape.*

Again, Lise's eyes fell on Anne Balfour; the older woman's face seemed taut with an expression the lady did not understand.

How did Mother convince her to go along with this? Did she take advantage of Anne's poor condition?

More shame flowed through her, and she forced herself to look at Xavier, who had not shifted his own eyes away from her face.

Father Callaway turned to the congregation.

"On this first day of March, in the year 1815, if any man do allege and declare any impediment why they may not be coupled together in matrimony, by God's law or the laws of this realm, and will be bound, and sufficient sureties with him, to the parties, or else put in a caution to prove his allegation, then the solemnization must be deferred until such time as the truth be tried."

With bated breath, Lise looked again toward the guests, who made no move to contest the validity of their union.

They should all cry out together in unison. Surely, everyone in this room has their doubts!

Yet only silence ensued, leaving the clergyman to continue.

"I require and charge you both, as ye will answer at the dreadful day of judgment when the secrets of all hearts shall be disclosed, that if either of you knows any impediment, why ye may not be lawfully joined together in matrimony, ye do now confess it. For be ye well assured, that so many as are coupled together otherwise than God's Word doth allow are not joined together by God, neither is their matrimony lawful," Father Callaway continued before turning to Xavier.

What of the marriage banns? Lise thought irrelevantly and suddenly she found herself wondering if the marriage was legitimate in any way. Could this all be a farce fabricated by her mother somehow?

She looked desperately at her mother, the confusion of wanting to be wed to Xavier and the desire to flee the hotel causing her dizziness.

"Xavier Balfour, wilt thou have this woman to be thy wedded wife, to live together after God's ordinance in the holy estate of matrimony? Wilt thou love her, comfort, honor, and keep her in sickness and in health, and, forsaking all other, keep thee only unto her, so long as ye both shall live?"

Xavier smiled lovingly, nodding as he spoke.

"I will."

The priest then turned to her, his rheumy eyes unblinking, and for a fleeting moment, Lise felt as if he could read the impurity in her soul.

"Elizabeth Burnaby of Holden, wilt thou have this man to be thy wedded husband, to live together after God's ordinance in the holy estate of matrimony? Wilt thou obey him, and serve him, love, honor, and keep him in sickness and in health, and, forsaking all other, keep thee only unto him, so long as ye both shall live?"

I will burn in hell for this. I am lying before God and the man I love.

"Elizabeth?"

"I will," she managed to breathe before she could blurt out the heaviness in her heart.

Xavier's registered relief as though he had worried that she would refuse.

"Xavier, I will have you repeat these words: I, Xavier Balfour, take thee, Elizabeth, to be my wedded wife, to have and to hold from this day forward, for better or worse, for richer or poorer, in sickness and in health, to love and to cherish, till death us do part, according to God's holy ordinance, and thereto I plight thee my troth."

Xavier repeated his vows easily and without forgetting one word, causing Lise to wonder if he had not memorized the Solemnization of Matrimony beforehand.

When Lise was asked to repeat the vows, she stumbled and stuttered, causing the guests to titter.

They find this endearing when the reality is much more devastating.

Xavier took hold of her left hand and stared deeply into her eyes as the minister spoke.

"After me, Xavier—"

But he was not granted the opportunity to finish as Xavier knew the words to be spoken as he slipped a golden band over Lise's ring finger.

"With this ring I thee wed, with my body I thee worship, and with all my worldly goods I thee endow, in the name of the Father, and of the Son, and of the Holy Ghost. Amen."

"Amen," Lise whispered, staring at the ring, a lump forming in her throat.

"Let us pray," Father Callaway intoned, and all lowered their heads as he led the prayer.

"Oh, eternal God, Creator and Preserver of all mankind, Giver of all spiritual grace, the Author of everlasting life, send Thy blessing upon Thy servants, this man and this woman, whom we bless in Thy name, that, as Isaac and Rebecca lived faithfully together, so these persons may surely perform and keep the vow and covenant betwixt them made and may ever remain in perfect love and peace together and live according to Thy laws, through Jesus Christ, our Lord. Amen."

Once again, the clergyman joined their hands together and nodded.

"Those whom God hath joined together, let no man put asunder."

The words caused a sob to escape Lise's lips, but no one heard it but Xavier, who mistook it for happiness.

It will not be a man who puts us asunder, Lise thought miserably. *It will be two ladies.*

CHAPTER TEN

Something stirred him in the night and Xavier blinked several times, his eyes adjusting to the darkness in which he was enshrouded.

It took him a moment to remember the festivities that had led him to be fast asleep in his marital bed.

There had been a small party for the shockingly tiny wedding, but Xavier had enjoyed himself regardless. That night was not the one for questioning his mother or the duchess about their planning.

Nor about why there was no man to give Lise away, either. There will be plenty of time for questions later. Tonight is for us and no one else.

Instinctively, he reached for his wife, but to his surprise, Lise was not at his side.

Awake now, Xavier cast the blankets aside and rose to look about for a sign of her.

"Lise?" he called, but there was nothing but the crackling of the fireplace to answer him. The light was dying out at the hearth, indicating that it was quite late, but it was not until he noticed the time on the desk clock that he realized precisely how late it was.

Where in God's name could she have gone at two o'clock in the night?

The wedding reception had been filled with wine and whiskey, but he and Lise had retired together well before the hour of ten, although he did not recall when he had fallen asleep. All he remembered for certain were the sweet hours he had spent with his wife in his arms.

For that time, he had been certain that she was finally content, their marriage sweeping away any doubts or fears she may have had, but finding himself alone made him reconsider his conclusion.

Donning a thick robe of wool, he found his slippers and headed into the cold hotel, shivering slightly beneath coarse material. He could not imagine what would inspire Lise to rise from the warmth of their bed.

In the hallway, he encountered the night concierge.

"Byron, have you seen Lady Elizabeth?" he demanded of the older man who shuffled through the fifth floor.

He seemed surprised to see Xavier.

"Mr. Xavier. I-I do not, sir. Could she be asleep?"

Xavier scoffed and brushed past the man.

"Clearly, she is not asleep if I am asking you," he snapped irritably. He made his way to the staircase, pausing on each floor to see if there was a sign of his wife, but there was no one to be seen.

He stopped in the lobby, pausing to light a candelabra to carry through the darkened dining room, but again, he was left disappointed.

Could she have gone to her mother?

It troubled him to think that, after the intimacy they had shared, she would flee to the duchess.

Yet there was little he could do but return to their bedchamber and hope she returned.

To his surprise, she was in the bed asleep when he arrived, and for an instant, he wondered if he had simply overlooked her.

His mind was still quite cloudy from the wine, but could he have made such a mistake?

Xavier hovered by her side and peered into her slumbering face, confusion overwhelming him as he did. She seemed to have been asleep for hours and she wore very little, just as the last time he had seen her, entrenched in his arms.

The excitement of the day has gotten the best of you, he decided. *I truly must rest.*

He climbed back into the bed and slid closer to her, relishing the feel of her breaths against him.

She is an angel, he thought joyously as sleep overcame him once more. *My own angel sent from the heavens.*

———

Lise sat at the toilet, brushing her long mass of curls, and Xavier watched her silently for a long moment before announcing his wakefulness.

"You truly are a vision," he sighed, and she turned to smile at him. Her face was much more relaxed than he had ever seen.

"You have already married me, my love. You need not flatter me for another moment," she replied jestingly as Xavier rose from the bed to kiss her forehead sweetly.

"It is not flattery if it is so," he replied. "Did you sleep well?"

"I had little say in the matter. With the events of yesterday, it was difficult to fight sleep."

"Do you fight with sleep?" Xavier asked.

"On occasion." Lise smiled warmly to take the seriousness from their discussion. "How did you sleep, darling?"

"You will jeer at me when I say," he replied, chuckling. "But I woke at the hour of two and searched the hotel for you."

Her eyes widened.

"You did what?"

"I must have had too much wine," he confessed, perching on the edge of the bed. "I was certain you were gone, and I looked about for you."

"You must have been dreaming!"

"No," Xavier laughed, feeling foolish as he read the dubious expression upon her face. "I spoke with Byron."

"My word!" Lise giggled.

"I would—"

An urgent knock at the door caused Xavier to look up in surprise.

"Who is there?"

"Mr. Xavier, Mr. Balfour requests your presence immediately," came Joshua's voice from the hallway.

Xavier's eyebrows rose.

"What is the meaning of this now?" he wondered, rising to dress.

"Mr. Xavier?" Joshua called.

"Yes, Joshua. Tell him I will be there in a moment."

"He..." Joshua cleared his throat.

"Oh, for the love of God, Joshua, do come in rather than yell from the corridor!" Xavier snapped impatiently. He gave his wife an apologetic look and closed the sliding doors so that she would not be embarrassed in her nightclothes.

"Forgive me, Mr. Xavier," Joshua muttered, lowering his eyes as he realized his employer's state of undress. "But he requests that you come at once and that you come alone."

"Who would I bring? The king?" Xavier scoffed, but instantly, he knew what his father was asking.

He wishes me to come without my wife.

The understanding infuriated Xavier.

"Sir?" Joshua pressed. "He is waiting on an answer."

"Tell him to hold his horses," Xavier barked back. "I will be along when I am presentable."

"Yes, Mr. Xavier."

Joshua scampered out of the suite to relay the message, and Xavier sauntered back into the bedchamber where Lise was already dressed.

"Your talents have no bounds!" he joked. "How did you manage your corset without an abigail?"

Yet Lise did not return his smile as she peered at her face in the mirror, brushing her long strands out of her face with impatience.

"Does your father oft call for urgent interviews at this hour of the morning?" she asked.

"I do believe this is a first," Xavier confessed, his brow furrowing slightly as he thought about it.

"The matter must be of great importance."

Her words were stiff, but Xavier was still considering what Charlton could need.

"I should get to him before he gives himself apoplexy. Will I see you in the dining room? We should discuss our honeymoon."

Lise smiled weakly at him.

"Yes," she whispered. "We will do that."

"Are you all right, Lise?" he asked, covering the distance between them. He cupped her face.

She is such a range of emotions. I will never understand her.

"Yes...Xavy?"

"Yes, my love?" To his surprise, tears had filled her eyes, but they remained unshed as she stared at his face. "Lise, what is it?"

"I-I want you to know that I truly do love you," she breathed.

"I love you also."

She pulled her head away and quickly shoved past him to head toward the door without another word.

"Lise?"

She paused but did not turn.

"I will see you at breakfast."

She opened the door and disappeared into the hallway without responding, filling his chest with tightness.

She is complicated and beautiful. It is a devastating combination.

He knew he could not leave his father waiting much longer, and he quickly dressed, making himself available in the office where his father paced about. Elias sat expressionless in a chair, and both sets of eyes rested on Xavier as he entered.

"Where is your key to the safe?" Charlton demanded without preamble. "I need it at once!"

Instinctively, Xavier reached into his waistcoat to retrieve it, but he remembered that he no longer had it.

"I-it is in my suite," he explained. "I will go for it."

"Bloody hell!" Charlton roared, slamming his fists down against the desk. "I knew it!"

Xavier stared at his father, perplexed.

"What is the issue, Father?" he demanded, glancing at Elias, who had leaned forward to rest his forehead against his steepled hands.

"*The issue?*" Charlton squeaked. His face was so red, Xavier was sincerely concerned for his health. "The issue is that there are thirty pounds missing from the safe. I do not suppose you know their where-abouts, do you?"

"You are losing your wits over a bookkeeping error? Xavier snapped back, his annoyance mounting. "My word, Father. Perhaps it is time for you to step down. You are under too much pressure."

"It is not an accompt error, Xavier," Elias said quietly. "I had noticed there was a discrepancy a month ago."

"Then why did you not say so then?"

"I did," Elias sighed. "To Charlton."

Slowly, Xavier raised his head and glared at both men.

"There was a problem with the accompts and you left me unawares? For what reason? Do you expect I took the money?"

The idea was laughable.

"No, of course not," Charlton grumbled. "We know you did not."

"Then what reason could you have for not telling me of this?"

"At first," Elias sighed, "we thought it was a simple error, but as more money vanished...ten pounds went last night alone."

"T-ten pounds?" Xavier choked. "Last night? Are you certain?"

"Eli and I have been counting every night. Whoever it is has been coming in the night when Byron is on his security rounds. The culprit knows the hotel well..."

Charlton cleared his throat.

"And obviously has a key."

Xavier's eyes bugged almost clear from his head.

"Mother?" he gasped, and both men groaned.

"I forewarned you, Charlton," Elias muttered. "He will not accept this."

"No! I cannot believe Mother would steal from us."

"It is not your mother, you fool!" Charlton barked. "It is your wife!"

A deep, heavy silence fell over the office, and Xavier heard a strange buzzing in his ears.

"Xavier, we know how much you care for her—" Elias started to say, but Xavier interrupted him by beginning to laugh.

"The daughter of a duke, stealing away in the night to steal pennies compared to her worth in the dukedom. And not just once for the thrill perhaps but several times? Do you hear how ludicrous that sounds?" Xavier spat out at them, but inside, his heart was racing.

Where did she go last night? It was she who suggested she take the key...

"No," Xavier said again flatly. He spun to rush from the office.

"Where are you going now?" Charlton yelled after him.

"I am going to speak to my wife!"

He dashed out of the lobby and into the dining room, but when he approached the table, Emmeline sat alone with the baby.

"Where are the duchess and Elizabeth?" he demanded. His sister looked up at him in surprise.

"I-I would not know," she replied. "I have not seen either one this morning."

She had barely finished speaking when Xavier made his way back through the servant's stairs to the fourth floor. He pounded on the duchess's chambers, but there was no response.

"Mr. Xavier, is there something I can do for you?" Antoinette asked, aroused by all the ruckus.

"I am looking for Her Grace of Holden and my wife. Have you seen them?"

Consternation twisted over the housekeeper's face.

"Her grace...she departed not fifteen minutes ago. I daresay that Lady Elizabeth was with her, Mr. Xavier."

"Departed for where? Luton?"

Antoinette paled more.

"N-no, Mr. Xavier. She had her trunks. I daresay she was returning to Holden."

The news made no sense to him, and he was certain Antoinette was mistaken.

"No!" he insisted. "You are wrong!"

He did not permit Antoinette an opportunity to respond, and he bounded up the stairs toward his own quarters again, bursting through the door. He froze in at the threshold, his heart in his throat.

Across the sitting room, his eyes fell on the writing desk where something glimmered against the cream of a paper sheet.

As if he was possessed by an unseen entity, he walked slowly toward the desk and read the only three words on the page, next to the safe key and the ruby heirloom ring.

Please forgive me.

CHAPTER ELEVEN

"It is not enough money," Patience whispered. "We will not get far enough away. We will be recognized and brought back!"

"What would you have me do, Mother?" Lise demanded miserably. "I was caught. There was no other way."

They sat together in the back of the stagecoach, speaking quietly as to not attract the attention of the other passengers. They were the only women, and their fine clothes seemed amiss in a hired coach, but Lise silently prayed that the journey to Colchester would go without incident.

"I know," Patience replied quietly. "You did right by coming for me. It is a blessing we were dressed."

Lise was glad her mother could find a blessing in all that had happened. In her mind, the entire plan had failed terribly.

I was promised more time! More time to collect money, more time to live in the hotel.

Yet she knew what troubled her the most. Her heart was shattered. She had never expected the reality of leaving to be as shocking as it had been, but there was no other choice.

I married Xavier and ruined his life.

There was certainly no going back. By then, her husband would certainly know the truth. The ring, the note, and the key were enough to make what had happened clear to him. He would undoubtedly go looking for her in Holden where her father would learn what she and her mother had done.

Perhaps they would find a way to annul the marriage, or perhaps Xavier would forever be tied to her, but it had all been for nothing.

The shame was unbearable, and without realizing it, Lise's face was stained with tears.

"You must not lose your wits now," the duchess hissed in her ear. "We must get as far away as possible without being seen."

"Yes, Mother," she sniffled. "I understand."

It was much easier said than done, and as the coach trotted away from Luton, Lise closed her eyes, willing herself to keep her composure.

"James will be terribly worried," Lise said after a long silence. "We must send him word that we are well."

"James is the least of our concerns," Patience replied sternly. "He could not be bothered to leave his wife to come."

Lise's eyes flew open, and she gaped at her mother.

"You stayed with Father alone for the month? Mother, you swore—"

"Lower your voice!"

Contritely, Lise did as she was told and inhaled deeply.

"Mother, you should not have done that. He could have killed you."

"He almost did—once again."

Gooseflesh prickled her arms, and Lise looked at her mother compassionately.

"You have endured so much yet remained so strong," she whispered. "How did you manage?"

Patience reached for her hand and squeezed it gently.

"God has a way of seeing you through the most difficult circumstances. Some are blessed with strong bodies, others with great wealth. God gave me the greatest gift of all."

Lise stared at her uncomprehendingly.

"He gave me a daughter, Lise. He bestowed you upon me, and He could not have given me anything better."

Lise grimaced.

"You do not believe me?" Patience asked. "There were many times before you were born, Lise, that I went to sleep and prayed that He take me in the night."

"Mother!"

"Of course, I would never do anything so drastic," she said quickly. "I was merely so unhappy at the brutish hands of your father, I sometimes begged for a quick end."

"Oh, Mother..."

"When James was born, I knew your father was pleased. He was gentler for a time, happy that I had given him a marquis for the duchy."

She smiled, a faraway look in her eyes as if she was in a better time.

"He did not strike out at me as much. I had hoped the worst was over."

She sighed.

"But, of course, I was naïve. Once you were conceived, the beatings began again. I nearly lost you twice because of his temper."

The information was horrific, and Lise wished Patience would stop, but it was clear that her mother needed to spill the terrible pain that had built inside her for years.

"Perhaps, in a terrible way, that made us closer, you and I, Lise. I would do anything to protect you, and somehow, I knew you were a girl before you were born. Sometimes, mothers know such things."

"I imagine," Lise murmured, her throat scratchy as she spoke. She feared she would burst into sobs.

"I always knew that James would survive his father. The duke doted on him, and when you were very small, he did on you, too. It was not until you became inquisitive, questioning his authority, that he realized that you were not going to be his submissive daughter forever. It infuriated him, but it gave me hope for the first time, Lise. I saw a fire inside you that I once had, and it inspired me to do better for both of us."

Lise felt as though she was looking at her mother with different eyes.

"I love your father," Patience continued. "Perhaps not in the romantic way that you love Xavier but I, too, understand the despair of knowing you lost your husband."

Pain pierced Lise's heart, and she squeezed Patience's hand tightly.

"I am sorry for what you had to endure for this," Patience whispered. "Know I did not want you to hurt after all your father has done to you."

"I know, Mama," Lise breathed. "I know."

Yet even with the duchess's heartfelt words, the explanation and the absolute certainty that all she said was true, nothing could take away the deep sense of loss in Lise's gut.

You must forsake Xavier and the Balfour Hotel. There is nothing that can be done to make this right. Going forward, it will simply be Mother and I against the world.

CHAPTER TWELVE

The horse neighed with irritation as Xavier dismounted, leaving Elias to hurry after him.

"Xavier, I do not think this is a sound idea. If they are here, which I doubt very much, the duchy guards will see you off."

"If you are concerned about your health, I suggest you remain back," Xavier hissed. "No one asked you to accompany me here."

"Contrary to your beliefs, Xavier, I am your comrade and your family. I would not leave you to confront the duke on your own."

"You are not my family!" Xavier snarled, whirling short of the gates. "You are merely the man who snaked his way into my family to steal away our hotel."

Elias gaped at him and laughed shortly.

"I had no idea that you felt this way," he said quietly. "But I assure you, that is hardly the case. I am a part of your family because I love your sister. I never had any interest in the hotel."

"A likely tale," Xavier growled. "One which can wait for another time."

He stalked toward the gates and pushed his way inside.

"Are you coming or not?" Xavier demanded.

"Of course, I am."

The men made their way up the pathway, leading toward Pine-haven, keenly aware of their surroundings.

"None of this makes sense," Xavier muttered. "Look at how she lived here. Why would she steal from us?"

He was speaking more to himself than his brother-in-law, but Elias answered.

"Perhaps the duchy has fallen upon hard times. Perhaps the duke sent her to do his bidding."

"The duke has been in absentia. I feel as though the duchess is the mastermind of this enterprise."

He thought of Lise's nearness, of her bright smile and sad eyes. It was impossible to reconcile that she had been acting, pretending to love him to steal a few pounds.

Unless she intended to steal more.

He realized that she had been there that morning when Joshua had announced his father demanded to see Xavier.

Perhaps we simply learned about her scheme too early.

"Who is there?" A liveried butler opened the door and peered speculatively at the duo. "Identify yourselves at once!"

"Mr. Xavier Balfour and Mr. Elias Compton of Luton. We have urgent business with the Duke of Holden."

"Is he expecting you?"

"He is not, but the matter pertains to Her Grace and Lady Elizabeth."

The butler's eyes widened.

"Do you know where they are?" he asked in a hushed voice, his watery eyes darting about nervously. "Are they well?"

Xavier and Elias exchanged a look and shook their heads in unison.

"We are also seeking their whereabouts," Xavier replied slowly. "Is the Duke available?"

"I will announce you," the old man replied, ushering them inside. "Remain here, please."

He shuffled away and they looked about the opulent foyer with interest.

"You see?" Xavier rasped. "There is much to sell here. There is no reason for such a theft."

"Perhaps that is how they afford so much luxury—thieving from unsuspecting households," Elias offered. Xavier glowered at him, but before he could respond, the butler returned.

"His Grace will see you," he mumbled but paused. The men looked at him expectantly.

"His Grace is rather...discontent today," the servant muttered, but there was no chance to ask what that could mean for he ambled off down the hall.

"*I* am discontent today," Xavier barked, and Elias grunted as they followed the butler.

"Your Grace," the ancient man said, bowing, "may I present Mr. Alexander Heartling and Mr. Elmer Crampus of Loughborough."

"Enter," the duke snapped, waving them inside.

"Forgive us, Your Grace. I am Xav—"

"I heard who you are. What I do not know is what you want," the Duke of Holden snarled. "Where are my wife and daughter?"

"Your Grace, I am Xavier Balfour," Xavier said to him, but the name seemed to mean nothing to the nobleman.

"How many times must we go through introductions? I asked you a question!"

Xavier cast Elias a sidelong look. The duke was a miserable character of poor disposition, but he seemed to have no idea who it was who stood before him.

"Your Grace, I am Lady Elizabeth's husband."

The duke's face twisted into a sneer as he looked at Xavier.

"Is this a joke?" he asked, looking to Elias. "I have not any time for such ridiculousness."

"It is not a joke, Your Grace, I assure you. Your wife and daughter have stolen a substantial sum from my hotel and fled, thereby abandoning the marital home."

Confusion quickly turned to ire, and the duke rose, slamming his fists against the desk to cause the contents atop to shake.

"What are you suggesting?" the duke hissed. "That my wife, the duchess, and my daughter are common criminals?"

"I suggest nothing. I came here hoping to confront my wife on the matter, but I can plainly see they would not return here."

"You are mad," the duke insisted but as he spoke. Xavier saw a cold terror falling over his face.

"If they do return, Your Grace, will you send word to the Balfour Hotel in Luton?"

The duke's head jerked up.

"I know of your hotel. I was there once many years ago."

"Then you will know where to send word," Xavier said curtly. "Good day."

He bowed and turned to leave with Elias on his heels.

"Do you believe him?" Elias asked. "It was difficult to tell with his causticness."

"I believe him. I think he is coming to the understanding that his wife has abandoned his marital home also."

"He is not a pleasant fellow, is he?"

"He is a horse's arse, but that is not my concern at the moment."

"What is your concern?" Elias demanded. "The money is not substantial. We will recover from that loss."

Xavier eyed him and shook his head.

"Do you think I care about the money?" he asked in disbelief. "My only concern is finding Lise and bringing her home."

Elias wisely closed his mouth as they mounted their horses, but Xavier did not need to be told what his brother-in-law was thinking.

He believes I am daft for chasing after her. Perhaps he is right.

Yet Xavier knew he would not rest until he looked his wife in the eye and learned why she had done it.

She cannot lie to me. I will know when I ask her face to face.

"Will we return to home?" Elias asked.

"No. We will go to Whittaker."

––––––––

James, the Marquis of Holden, lived in Holden with his wife, Lady Lydia. While his father was brash and rude, Lord Holden was much more amiable with a softer tone and concerned eyes of chocolate.

He looked very little like his sister, but neither sibling seemed to resemble either parent.

"My word, you cannot be sincere!" Lady Holden cried in disbelief. "Have they run off together then?"

"We cannot be certain, but it appears so," Xavier muttered, disappointed that they had not found the pair with the marquis.

"This does not sound like anything my sister could do," Lord Holden insisted. "Are you certain they are not simply imposters, pretending to be my mother and sister?"

"Quite," Elias sighed. "We performed our due diligence upon the engagement."

"Obviously not well enough if neither I nor my father was invited to the wedding!"

Xavier flushed at the reminder of how blindly he had allowed Lise into his life.

"I cannot fault them," Lady Holden announced, setting her teacup against the table with a firm smash. "Your father—"

"That is quite enough, my lady," James interrupted, his face turning as red as Xavier's.

"What of the duke?" Elias pressed, unabashed. "Please, if it will help bring them home…"

He stared imploringly at the couple.

"You will not bring them home if they are running," Lydia said flatly, and again her husband gave her a scathing look.

"Why is that?" Xavier asked. Only silence met his question, and his frustration mounted.

"Please! This was not a scheme for me! She is my wife, whether or not she believed that when she married me. I deserve to know why she would do this, particularly if this is out of character for her."

Lydia and James exchanged a long look, but it was James who spoke this time.

"My father has a rather infamous temper," the marquis muttered.

"He is a brute and a bully," Lydia added despite James' withering gaze.

"If Mother and Lise would not provoke him, he would not be forced to use his fists so freely," James growled.

"Are you suggesting they took the money because the duke beats them?"

Lydia nodded slowly.

"It is the only explanation I can imagine. The duchy is very well off. There is no need to steal. It seems they had concocted an elaborate ruse to ensure they were not easily found by our peers," she offered, and Xavier felt sick to his stomach.

Or did my mother arrange for all this in her psychosis?

It was impossible to know who had gotten the matter underway.

"How much was taken from your hotel, Mr. Balfour? I would like to reimburse you," Lord Holden sighed, nodding toward his manservant, but Xavier was already on his feet and moving toward the door.

"That is a matter for me and my wife," he said grimly. "I thank you for your time and candor. Come along, Mr. Compton."

"Where are we going now, Xavier? It is getting dark."

"We are going home," Xavier sighed. There was only one last person with whom to speak.

His mother.

———

Anne was dancing with herself when Xavier entered her bedchambers.

"Oh, darling!" she laughed. "I thought you would never come. When will we have a party again? Your reception was so lovely."

"Mother, where did the duchess go?" he demanded. "I know you and she have spent a great deal of time together."

The smile faded from Anne's face, and she stared at him in surprise.

"Go?" she echoed. "She is not going anywhere. She is staying right here at the hotel, away from that wretched husband, who beats upon her and her daughter."

Xavier's mouth gaped open.

"You knew of that?" he choked.

"Of what?"

"Mother! You must stay focused and tell me what you discussed with the duchess."

Anne's brow furrowed slightly and she sank onto her bed, her white nightgown spread around her.

"She was looking so forward to your wedding," Anne recalled, reaching toward the vanity with trembling hands. Her fingers closed around a wine glass, and she gulped back a big sip before continuing.

"It was why I chose her," she whispered slyly, leaning in as if disclosing a big secret. "She loathes her husband as much as I loathe mine."

"Mother!"

Anne snickered and took another sip of wine, plopping the glass unceremoniously back onto the desk. She grinned almost lewdly at her son.

"Do not tell me you have been visiting the brothels again and your wife has left you already."

"Mother, the duchess and Elizabeth have run away. Do you know where they might have gone?"

Anne's face crumpled, and she shook her head.

"No," she slurred. "They would not run off. I promised Patience that she would be safe here."

"Safe from the duke?"

"Why would she go? Did your father send them away?"

"No, Mother," he sighed, but to his dismay, large tears filled Anne's drunken eyes.

"She was my friend," Anne moaned in the most heartbreaking manner. "Why did she leave? What happened?"

"I think she was afraid of the duke, Mother," Xavier muttered, the sad reality of what had truly happened washing through him in a torrent.

"Men ruin us all," Anne muttered, curling onto her side as tears slipped down her face. She seemed very much a small child at that moment, but Xavier wished he, too, could do the same.

He had lost his wife even before he knew who she was, truly.

I did not ask. I knew something troubled her from the first day I laid eyes upon her, yet I did nothing.

Suddenly, Xavier was furious. He was furious with his mother for withholding the information, furious with the duke for scaring her away, furious with the duchess for arranging such a plan.

Yet, above all, Xavier was furious with himself for allowing it all to occur the way it had.

Now she is long gone, and you will never see her again.

CHAPTER THIRTEEN

"You may escape his wrath, Lise, but I will not. I cannot return to Luton with you."

The echo of her mother's voice caused her heart to twist with every replay of the words as the coach made its way through the countryside toward the place where she swore she would never return.

It was difficult to believe that four months had passed since she had last been in Luton, but the sweetness of early summer tantalized her nose, and she knew she was not dreaming the feeling of sick anticipation in her stomach.

Luton loomed beyond, and for a fleeting moment, Lise considered riding onward, but she had only paid enough to get her that far.

It had been a harrowing four months, the constant moving about, the nagging fear of being seen and reported. From town to town they moved, finding odd jobs where they could but never staying anywhere for longer than a fortnight.

"Mother, we cannot keep running," Lise told her miserably. "We have little money, and I am growing weary."

"We cannot return," Patience told her with just as much conviction. "We have been gone two months. There is no excuse for it. He will murder us both."

"What if we return to Luton and beg the Balfours for help," Lise implored her, a wave of dizziness striking her. "At this rate, we will find ourselves in a grave regardless."

The duchess scoffed at her.

"How do you think those without manor houses live, child? We will find our own way somehow."

"They live with husbands who provide a living for them. I have no issue with the work, but we cannot find stability if we are constantly moving!"

It was an argument they would have for another month.

But now there was nothing left to fight about, and as the coach slowed, Lise reluctantly rose to leave.

"Have you someone meeting you, Miss?" the coachman asked.

"I am going to the Balfour Hotel," she replied dully. Saying the words aloud only caused her more anxiousness. The driver eyed her scornfully.

"No disrespect, Miss, but their standards are quite high for their employees. I daresay, if you are seeking employment as a chamber-maid, you should pretty yourself up some."

"Duly noted," Lise muttered, reaching for her trunk. She grimaced at the weight and paused to look around.

"Lady Elizabeth?"

Her heart thudded at the sound of her name, and she turned as a young man hurried toward her, a wide smile on his face. The coachman overheard this.

"Off with you now," the driver yelled. "Do not harass the women."

"It is all right," Lise assured him. "I know him."

She smiled wanly at Joshua.

"Hello, Joshua."

"I cannot believe it is you! Are you well? Here, permit me to take that."

He reached for her trunk, and she shot him a grateful look.

"Where are you going? I will tell no one I saw you if you prefer," he gushed looking about as though he worried they were being watched.

"I am going to the hotel to see my husband," she replied. Joshua balked.

"Are you?" he asked slowly. "I-I will see you there. I have a wagon. I have come to pick up supplies."

"You are truly an angel today, Joshua. Thank you."

"Does Mr. Xavier know you are coming?" he asked, and Lise shook her unkempt head of hair.

"He does not. Do you think he will handle the surprise well?"

Joshua gaped at her, pausing his gait to stare at her.

"My lady, he has been beside himself since you left. I do not know the details, of course, but he has hired men to search for you."

"I do not think he will be happy to see me," Lise confessed. "Not in the least."

"If you forgive me saying so, my lady, I think you are mistaken. I have never seen Mr. Xavier as smitten with anyone as he was with you."

A hot blush touched her cheeks, and she lowered her gaze to the dirt at her feet.

"I hope you are correct, Joshua," she murmured.

"My friends call me Josh," he whispered, grinning as he threw her trunk onto his waiting cart.

She beamed.

"Mine call me Lise," she replied quietly.

———

Matthew, the concierge turned red, white, and pink when he saw Lise enter the lobby.

"L-Lady Elizabeth!" he choked. "H-h-how do you do?"

"I have been much better, Matthew," she told him earnestly. "Would you know where I might find my husband?"

"He is in the office, in fact."

Lise tensed.

"Is he alone?"

"Yes, my lady."

She exhaled with relief. She was not sure she had the strength to endure Elias or Charlton, not when she had so much to discuss with Xavier.

"Permit me to announce you, Lady Elizabeth."

"Of course."

They cannot have the thief alone in the office, after all.

Matthew hurried to knock on the door, stealing fully inside and closing the door at his back.

He was barely in when the door opened again and Xavier stood in the doorway, gaping in shock.

"Lise!" he choked. "It is you!"

"Hello, Xavier."

She lowered her head in embarrassment, knowing that she must look affrighting, but there was little she could do.

"I realize you have many questions, and I will do my best—"

"I have many questions," he agreed, striding toward her, and she braced herself for a slap or cruel words. To her amazement, she was swept into his arm, his face buried into the tangled mess of her hair.

"Why did you not tell me?" he murmured. "Why did you run off?"

Stunned, she looked at him, shaking her head.

"I-I do not know what you mean," she muttered. "I am sorry about the money."

"Come inside the office," he said, realizing that everyone about them had stopped to stare.

She followed him as he barked at Matthew to see her trunk up to their suite.

"Have the abigails wash and iron all her dresses," he instructed. Lise shook her head vehemently.

"No!" she cried. "I-I cannot stay. I must go back to my mother..."

Xavier closed the door and shook his sandy head of hair.

"No, darling, you do not," he promised. "You are safe here. You always were."

"You do not understand," she moaned, but she could not comprehend why he was handling her return so well.

"I do understand, and I am so glad you have returned. I know about the duke. I know what you and your mother planned."

"H-how?" she demanded. "Who could have possibly told you?"

"Your sister-in-law, Lady Holden."

"Lydia!" Lise breathed. She would never have expected James to speak against the duke, but she had not thought of the outspoken Lydia.

"So you see? All is well. Tell me where the duchess has gone, and I will send a coach for her."

"No!" Lise sighed. "She will not come back. The duke will...he will never permit her to stay. He will not permit me to stay, either."

Xavier blinked and looked at her in confusion.

"The duke has died, Lise."

The words were shockingly fulfilling and devastating simultaneously. Lise did not know which emotion to deal with first.

"Dead?" she repeated. "How?"

"It was a terrible, freakish accident," Xavier explained vaguely. "One of those blasted things."

Lise's mouth opened and closed as she tried to understand what she had just been told.

"An accident?"

"So they say," Xavier replied with too much brightness. "I had thought that was why you had returned. So you see? There is no reason to stay away. He is no longer a threat. The duchess, or rather, the dowager duchess, is free to return."

"Are you certain, Xavy? He is dead? You have seen his body?"

"Your brother is already the new Duke of Holden, Lise. I can send him word also that you have returned."

Without warning, a sob escaped her lips, and she buried her hands in her face with humiliation.

"I am sorry!" she gasped but Xavier wrapped her trembling body in his arms and shushed her gently.

"You need not be sorry. You were afraid," he murmured. "I only wish you had come to me first."

"I did not expect to fall in love with you, Xavier!"

"I did not expect to fall in love with you, either, Lise. But I have— desperately, madly, and completely in love with you. I've prayed day and night for your return."

She raised her head to look into his face, tears streaking her face. He reached into his breast pocket to hand her a handkerchief, and she dabbed at her cheeks hastily.

"But, I do want to know one thing, my dear," Xavier said once she had caught her breath. "If you did not intend to stay and you did not know about your father, why did you come back?"

She bit on her lower lip and sniffled, pulling herself out of his arms.

"I am with child," she replied, placing his hands against her swollen belly. Xavier's eyes widened in shock.

"What?"

She nodded and smiled.

"It appears that you will have your sons, after all."

"I would be just as content with a beautiful, ebony-haired daughter with porcelain skin just like her mother."

Lise's body sagged against her husband, and she shook her head as more tears streamed from her eyes.

"I do not deserve you," she whispered.

"You do, my lady, and I deserve you."

He turned away, his hand on her as he led her toward the desk. From inside, he withdrew both her wedding ring and the ruby, sliding them onto her shaking finger.

"If you should ever feel the need to take these off again," he murmured. "I would hope you leave me with a better note than the one you left me."

She blinked and shook her head, swallowing the grittiness in her throat.

"I will never feel the need to remove them again because I did not ever wish to take them off at all. I always wished to be married to you, Xavy."

He smiled and brushed his lips over her forehead.

"I know," he said softly. "That is how I knew you would always return to me."

EPILOGUE

"I do not recall the summer ever being so hot," Lise complained, reaching for a fan from the table. Emmeline giggled.

"I, too, was with child in the summer, and it does feel much hotter, I concur."

The women exchanged a smile and darted their eyes toward the lawn where their husbands were engaged in a fencing exchange as the guests watched appreciatively.

"If this were a year ago," Emmeline confessed, "I would think they were doing that to end each other, not for sport."

"They seem to be getting along better," Lise agreed, settling back against the cushions to rest her hands on her belly.

"I daresay everyone is getting along better with my brother since you have come along, Lise," Emmeline chuckled. "I cannot say how you managed, but you did tame a beast."

Lise's smile faded.

"Xavier is not a beast!" she said sharply. "There is nothing beastly about him, even on his worst day."

"Forgive me, Lise. I know your father was rather cruel."

A short silence hung between them until Lise looked up at Emmeline's classically lovely face.

"Do you know what happened to my father?" she asked quietly. A small part of her did not wish to pursue the issue, but there were so many strange questions that could not be answered. A terrible spill the duke had taken down the stairs inside the manor, only to impale himself on one of his prized statues, which laid on the floor at the bottom. The surgeon claimed he had lain there bleeding for hours before eventually succumbing to his death.

Why was there a statue at the bottom of the stairs? Where were all the servants? How does such a thing happen?

Yet the matter was closed, and no one seemed the least bit concerned.

He had more enemies than friends. If someone were to have murdered him, no one would speak against it.

Lise freely admitted that she found his passing a relief, but the man was still her father.

"I only know what I have heard," Emmeline replied. "Gruesome details."

She shuddered and looked at Catherine cooing on a nearby blanket.

"It is why I insist that the stairs be carpeted. It will do well for your child, too."

Emmeline raised her eyes, her mouth thinning slightly when they rested on a pair of ladies in the courtyard, the duchess and Anne, laughing and whispering to each other as though they were schoolchildren.

"And it will help my mother when she is tripping about also."

"She is also much better," Lise said quickly. "I do not find her as reclusive as she was when I arrived."

"Perhaps," Emmeline sighed. "Your mother has been a godsend. I have never seen my mother so happy."

"We all require companions, Emmy," Lise replied softly. "Life can be dismally lonely."

"You have a kind heart, Lise. I am happy that you and Xavier have each other."

"I am blessed to have found a decent family along the way."

A soft smile formed on Emmeline's lips, which caused Lise to beam, too.

And, for the first time in a long while, they were happy, all of them, in the splendid Balfour Hotel.

———

Next book: The Mysterious Death of the Duke

I'd like to thank you for reading this book. I hope you enjoyed it.

Please view my other titles at:
https://books2read.com/amandadavis

Printed in Great Britain
by Amazon

41414002R00067